THE ARROWHEAD
CATTLE COMPANY

Also by Richard Clarke

THE PERALTA COUNTRY
THE HOMESTEADERS
THE COPPERDUST HILLS

THE ARROWHEAD CATTLE COMPANY

Richard Clarke

Walker and Company
New York

First published in the United States of America in 1988 by the
Walker Publishing Company, Inc.

Published simultaneously in Canada by Thomas Allen & Son
Canada, Limited, Markham, Ontario.

Library of Congress Cataloging-in-Publication Data

Paine, Lauran.
    The Arrowhead Cattle Company.

 I. Title.
PS3566.A34A89 1988   813'.54   88-20
ISBN 0-8027-4079-0

Printed in the United States of America

10 9 8 7 6 5 4 3 2 1

Contents

CHAPTER 1

A Big Full House

PORTERVILLE was one of those towns that mushroomed out of the campfires and log-mud structures that straddled a pair of wagon ruts going to and from the buffalo country. With the passing of the bison, Porterville's trading post fell on hard times. Freighters and a trickle of immigrants used the road to pass through—a few stopped to stock up, fewer still lingered long enough to support the post's inventory. So when an Easterner named Charles Haverhill came along, liked the open country with its backdrop mountains of awesome depth and height, and made a half-joking very low offer to buy the trading post, its founder snapped up the offer, packed his mules, loaded his squaw and pups on horses, and headed for Idaho.

Haverhill cut back the inventory, expanded his services to include wagon and buggy repair, blacksmithing, and a combination saloon and card room. Business picked up. Twelve years later Porterville—now called Haverhill—had passed from being a village to a town, the hundreds of miles of grassland round about filled up with cattle, and Charley Haverhill prospered.

He made some money off the range riders heading north in springtime and returning southward during autumn. But he did not make a lot of money from the rangemen because they drew very low wages and did not have much money. Charley's income was augmented by his percentage from the card room, which was frequented by riders, travelers passing through, freighters, and local players.

The card room did a modest business during summertime. It did better during late autumn and winter, when winds blew cold air straight from the perpetually ice-covered high peaks of the northward mountains. All Haverhill had to do was make sure that spittoons were handy, there were decks of cards, chips, and whiskey available, and have one of his employees keep the big pot-bellied cannon heater in the center of the room burning on cold and blustery nights.

The town had drifters, as every plains town did. Men of nondescript appearance, blown in like autumn leaves, and blown out the same way—some remaining for a few days, some for a couple of weeks, but none willing to remain unless they found work. Springtime, it was easier to find work with the cow outfits than in town, where every available job had been filled during summer months. Drifting rangemen on their way to warmer areas in autumn very rarely lingered, even if work was offered to them. They belonged to a unique brotherhood of chronic drifters. There were things that could incite them to remain in snow country, but for the most part the men continued to ride south. Their motivation, like that of birds and other creatures, was to get as far south as quickly as possible.

Autumn bad weather sometimes made drifters hole up for days or weeks at a time. A sudden cold spell, days of icy rain—sometimes there even was a brisk early snowfall. It was the biting cold straight off those distant ice fields that made men seek shelter where there was warmth, and while Charley's saloon fit the bill, a man could not spend every day drinking—not for a week, if it took that long for storms to pass. So they usually drifted into the card room.

Charley Haverhill did not employ professional gamblers. His place was strictly for social gamesters. Upon the rare occasions when professional card sharks had appeared, Charley and the town marshal made sure they were on the first stage leaving town.

There had never been a fight in Charley's card room. He intended to keep it like that. If some cowman in his cups got cranky, he was forcibly escorted to the roadway. Charley kept a benign, almost paternal, eye on his card room with its elegant maroon velvet draperies, its genuine wool carpeting, and its imported chandeliers with their many-faceted glass bangles to catch and reflect bright lamp glow.

The room was a genuine shock to most of the drifters who entered it for the first time. It was surprisingly elegant in a part of the country where probably nothing like it existed this side of the Barbary Coast. His card room was Charley Haverhill's pride and delight. There was also a tacit understanding by its users that Charley had not spent all that money to provide loafers with an elegant place to sit in out of storms. If they sat too long, one of Charley's barmen (all of whom wore maroon sleeve garters and were large, capable individuals) would suggest that they buy into one of the games or go sit in the saloon.

If any spectacular winnings or losses had ever occurred in the card room, no one could recall them. Especially the losses. Charley did not like that kind of publicity.

But there had indeed been a few interesting games. One bleak day when storm clouds were accumulating a compact, gray-eyed rider named Ben Moore showed up. After having a couple of jolts at the bar, and mostly out of curiosity, he drifted into the card room.

There was one table of Pedro and three poker games going. There was also a fragrant cloud of tobacco smoke hanging about shoulder high. With a couple of exceptions, all the players were stockmen. One of the exceptions was the town constable, a large, thick, ham-handed and bull-necked individual who chewed on his cigars, but never lighted them.

Ben Moore was invited to fill the chair of a poker player who had cashed in and departed. Opposite Ben was a weathered man of indeterminant years, gray as a badger, who smoked a little pipe and did not say a word, even when he made a discard; for replacement cards he nodded his head once, twice, three times for the number of cards he would draw.

The other three players were cattlemen, florid, thin-lipped, hard-eyed individuals who occasionally ordered drinks, made wry jokes, or sat for long, silent moments studying their cards and the faces of the other players before arriving at their decisions whether to drop out or up the pot.

For the stockmen, the game—the card room itself, the whiskey and cigars—was part of a particular ritual. It was not this way for the old man, who never spoke, or for Ben Moore. Ben bought in to be warm and pleasantly occupied. It was not clear why the old man was playing, but by his appearance, he was not someone who could afford to gamble, and certainly not to lose.

But he did lose. Occasionally he won a pot, but halfway into the second hour the old man's moderate good luck started to fail. The cattlemen eyed him dispassionately. As his stack of chips dwindled, the cattlemen closed for the kill. They baited him into three straight losses, then set him up for the final loss, the one that would cost him his last chip.

Ben had openers, a pair of kings. That was all he had. The cattlemen drew cards, made intent studies of their hands, then one of them pushed in a stack of chips he knew the old man could not match and smiled broadly around his cigar.

Ben drew three cards, could not build on them, and dropped out. The cattlemen were watching the old man, who finally removed the pipe and spoke as he pushed in his last chip and removed an old folded paper from an inside pocket and tossed it into the pot. "Two thousand acres of grassland five hundred miles south of here, clean and clear. Buildings ain't much." He nodded at the pot. "Worth more'n is in there."

The cattlemen flicked glances at one another. Ben thought two of them were going to balk. The third man leaned to expectorate into the brass spittoon, then straightened up nodding. He said, "Raise you, mister."

The old man watched the cowman shove in his chips, looked across at Ben, then hitched around, brought out an old leather purse, dug out matching value in gold coins and waited for the other two stockmen to come in. When they did the old man put aside the old purse, picked up his cards, sucked on his pipe, then said, "Call you, gents," and spread his cards face up and fanwise. He had a royal flush.

The cowman sat stunned, looking at the fanned-out cards. The man who had made the raise got red in the face. Ben watched the old man rake in his winnings, the largest pot since Ben had sat in.

Two of the cowmen dropped out and went to the barroom, leaving Ben, the old man, and the red-faced stockman, who was a very stubborn individual. As the old man's luck held, he whittled away at the cowman's holdings until he wiped him out completely. Then the lone cowman arose—sweating, furious, red as a beet—and also stamped out to the bar.

Ben and the old man settled down to play poker. Ben lost three pots in a row. The old man's expression never changed, he did not speak, except once when he met Ben's gaze with a hint of a crinkle around his eyes as he said, "Partner, you got to know when to fold, when to raise, when to stay out."

After that Ben won four pots in a row and the old man did not look across the table again or make a sound. He puffed on his pipe and lost three more hands.

Ben would have quit, but quitting when winning is a delicate business, and the old man gave no hint of being ready to concede.

Ben wiped him out, except for the grasslands deed and a few gold coins. When the old man tossed the deed into the pot, Ben eyed the piece of folded paper with misgivings, remembering what had happened the last time it had been put up. He had won around six hundred dollars, more than he had made all summer on the range.

Reluctantly, Ben pushed in two stacks of chips and watched the old man deal cards. His first two cards were a pair of jacks. His next three cards were all kings. He held his breath as he studied the old man's face. But it was as unreadable as a stone wall.

The old man finally raised faded blue eyes and placed a small stack of gold coins next to the land deed and waited. Ben's stomach was knotted as he also maintained an expressionless face and pushed in chips, plus one, and called.

The old man did as he had done earlier: he spread his cards face up and fanwise. He had three queens.

Ben let his breath out very slowly, put his cards face up and watched the old man's features crumple, his color go ashen.

As Ben raked in his pot the old man relighted his old pipe with unsteady hands. Ben picked up the deed, examined it casually and said, "Five hundred miles south—near a town?"

The old man's answer was toneless. "Not real near. The town's called Wileyville . . . about six, seven miles from the land." He pushed back to arise and had to hold onto the edge of the table when he was upright.

Ben pocketed the paper, dropped the chips into his hat to be cashed in and hefted the little stack of gold coins while watching the old man. He walked around the table, steadied the old man with his right hand and dropped the coins into the old man's threadbare coat pocket with his left hand. As he stepped back he said, "I was on my way south anyway. I might as well ride to Wileyville and see what I won."

"You won it fair and square," the old man muttered and walked in the direction of the barroom. After Ben had cashed in his chips he went looking for the old man, to buy him a drink, but he was gone.

He asked the cattlemen, who were standing unhappily together at the bar, who the old man was and where he lived. None of them knew anything about him. Neither did the barman.

Ben had a drink, then buttoned up to the throat and walked out into the blustery night. Every star was pegged into place, the sky was like obsidian, and the fierce north wind was down to frigid blasts now. As Ben headed for the livery barn to sleep in the hay, he knew from experience that although tomorrow would be clear and sunny, it would also be very cold.

He had gone into that poker game with twenty-seven dollars. He was too prudent by nature to be much of a gambler. His intention had been to win or lose perhaps ten dollars, then leave.

As he was burrowing into the hay, his intense pleasure at winning so much money was tempered by remembering the face of the old man who had lost so much, including a parcel of land that was five hundred miles south.

He considered lying over for a few days to try and find the old man. He had the time; he had no particular destination anyway, as long as he got south before winter really arrived.

In the morning as he was finishing breakfast at the local café, a rangeman walked in stamping his feet and wearing a skiff of snow on his hat. At Ben's glance, the cowboy sank down at the counter, called for coffee, looked at Ben with a wag of his head and said, "She's comin', partner. Snow clouds up over them northward mountains as thick as smoke. By evenin' we'll have six, maybe eight inches."

Ben paid up, hiked down to the livery barn, settled up, rigged out his muscled-up buckskin horse and rode southward, hoping to stay well ahead of the storm.

CHAPTER 2

A New Place

Wileyville was cold, but not windy. Its distant backdrop mountains had snow only at their uppermost topouts, where it remained as much as seven months out of the year.

The town was a pleasant, busy place with old trees shading both sides of Main Street. It had several buildings of red brick. It also had a fine Methodist church, painted white all the way up to the bell tower.

Wileyville was one of those places with a sense of permanence to it. As Ben Moore's buckskin horse walked in the direction of the livery barn at the lower end of town, his (and his rider's) interest in the town fairly well obliterated from memory the long, often hard and arduous traveling that had been required to get here.

The genial fat man who owned the livery barn and whose name was Henry Bullerman had been dealing wtih the public most of his adult life. As a result of this, plus his inherent interest in two-legged as well as four-legged creatures, Henry Bullerman had developed an ability to make pretty damned good judgments. He liked the buckskin's rider, a man with graying temples, whose boots were scuffed and run-over, and whose old trousers and shirt beneath the blanket-coat had been beaten against creekside rocks until they were a uniformly faded powder-blue color.

Henry pointed out the café. He leaned to also point out the rooming house. Finally, as he stood holding the buckskin's reins he jutted his chin in the direction of the saloon as he said, "There are two of 'em. That big place yonder across the road—it's owned by a man named Joseph Benour." The fat man fixed Ben with his gaze. "It's pronounced

8

'been-hour.' I tell you that, friend, because Joe is big and fast-tempered an' specially sensitive about how his name is pronounced."

Ben was tugging off his gloves as he nodded. He was careful not to smile as he replied to the fat man, "I'm obliged to you for warning me."

With that topic out of the way, the fat liveryman eyed Ben. "Been a while on the road, eh?"

"Five hundred miles' worth. Mister—?"

"Henry Bullerman."

"I'm Ben Moore, Mister Bullerman."

The fat man nodded, then looked pained. "Henry. There ain't many 'misters' in Wileyville. Maybe Mister Custis, who runs the bank, and sometimes Mister Bulow, who owns the big general store. . . . Sometimes I've heard Job Upton, who's got the stage and local freightin' franchise, called mister. Me, I'm just Henry. It don't rightly fit a man in his fifties, fat as a hawg with dang little hair, but what can a man do once his momma hangs a name on him?"

Ben smiled. "Well, now," he said, "I expect you were a real pretty baby, Henry," and they both laughed.

Henry would have led the horse back down the runway to be cared for but Ben stopped him by producing a limp piece of paper that he unfolded very carefully and held out for Henry Bullerman to scan, which Henry did—first out of curiosity, then again with a gathering scowl.

Ben refolded the paper very carefully, pocketed it and gazed at the liveryman. "You got any idea where that land is?"

Henry turned his head, looked up and down the road; looked back and cleared his throat. "Well, yes. I been in this country eleven years. There's a lot of folks been here longer, but eleven years is long enough to know a few things—and that piece of paper made out to a man named Frederick Oakley had ought to be worth maybe as much as two, three hunnert dollars."

A little scurrying cold wind was stirring dust in the road-way; Ben buttoned his old coat. "Who'd it be worth that much to, Henry?"

The liveryman made a narrow-eyed examination of the man in front of him before speaking again, and he avoided a direct answer to the question by saying, "Tell me somethin' that's none of my damned business, Ben: where did you get that land deed?"

"Won it in a poker game up north."

"Uh huh . . . well, it's been signed off, but before it's worth a damn you got to head for the county seat an' have it certified an' all, then they'll enter it into the books that you're the new legal owner. . . . You ever done anything like that before?"

Moore shook his head. "Never have. Never owned anything much before, except my outfit."

Henry did not seem as eager to take care of the buckskin horse now as he had been ten minutes earlier. He had his head barely cocked to one side as he eyed Ben Moore before asking his next question. "You figure on settling in out there?"

Ben's gaze had wandered to the steamy café window. He was hungry enough to eat a rattler if someone would hold its head. "I don't know," he said. "I got no idea what's out there." He smiled at the fat man and shrugged thick, sloping shoulders. "I never been real lucky, Henry. When a man's like that, he don't really expect much. I don't expect that piece of land to be much."

"You goin' over to the county seat to record that deed?"

"First off, I'm goin' to ride out and see what's out there. . . . See you in the morning, Henry. I'd like to get to the café before he locks up."

As Ben was scuffing through the dust Henry called after him. "Ain't a 'he,' it's a 'she.' "

Because a little gust of wind rattled through town heading southward, Ben Moore may not have heard Henry's last comment. It did not matter. The moment he pushed in out of the wind, smelled the tantalizing fragrance of cooking and saw the black-headed woman behind the counter raise black eyes as the door opened and closed, he knew for himself that the Wileyville caféman was no man.

Dusk was approaching even though it was little more than mid-afternoon, and by a rangeman's rule of thumb early darkness meant a storm.

There were three men along the café counter. It actually was a couple of hours early for supper. The woman came down and stared steadily at Ben as she mentioned a choice of roast beef, fried beef, beef stew, or pork meat with spuds and applesauce.

Her features were almost perfect. They were also expressionless. If she smiled, she probably did not do it often, and perhaps never at all to men. It was not hostility Ben sensed in her, it was rock-hard carefulness.

He watched her walk back beyond a hanging drapery. She was muscular, erect, had an easy, direct stride; she was very, very handsome. Not pretty—pretty went with sixteen to maybe eighteen or nineteen. Handsome was something folks didn't become until they were well into their twenties, at the very least. Ben guessed the handsome proprietor of the Wileyville café was about five to seven years younger than he was. Ben was forty.

He considered the other diners. Two were old gaffers, probably with shacks somewhere around town. The third man was tall, well above six feet, and sinewy but with a big rawboned frame. He had slightly high, flat cheekbones, a faint copperlike tint to his skin as though he spent all his time out of doors, and when he turned to reach for the coffee cup, Ben saw the badge on his shirt where the coat fell away.

Outside, a gust of wind came and went, occasionally rattling loose roofing and pelting the front window of the café with tiny particles of stone.

Ben ignored it and concentrated on his supper. In his experience that kind of a wind played itself out within a couple of hours.

The woman was a surprisingly good cook. Surprising because most towns such as Wileyville whose economies were kept primed by local stockmen had broken-down old trail cooks running their cafés. Occasionally those men were disagreeable, crippled up, indifferent about the quality of their cooking. Not all cafés were that bad but enough were to impress on drifting rangemen like Ben Moore that what they were going to get in a town café was about the same as they had got on trails, at marking-grounds, or even in the yards of cow outfits where there were no women.

Ben finished, paid up and went out front to stand in gathering gloom for a moment. There were a few store lights along Main Street, but they were winking out as Ben leaned on an overhang upright to build and light a smoke.

That very tall rawboned man with the badge came ambling northward on his final round of the day and stopped to drag a sulphur match across his raised leg and hold the furiously smoking match to Ben's cigarette. Afterward, he grinned. "That's part of our community welcomin' ritual," he said and laughed as Ben's face showed a broad smile.

"Well, sir, in that case," Ben said, "I got to tell you I've been in a lot of towns, but this here is the first one I ever saw that welcomed strangers. Mostly they watch you like a hawk, an' whether you do anything or not, they don't take to you for maybe ten years."

The lawman lingered, gazing out into the roadway as a pair of riders walked their horses past in the direction of the saloon that belonged to that man with the quick temper. He laughed as he turned his head toward Ben. "Yeah, I know how that is. First, they're suspicious of you. Then they decide there's something they don't like—color of your hair, maybe. . . . Couple of years later one or two comes up an' makes friends. Couple more years, a few more. . . .

Ben's eyes twinkled in the gloom. "Yeah . . . how long you been in Wileyville, Marshal?"

"Nine years," stated the tall man, flashing even, white teeth in the increasing darkness.

Ben heard the café doorlatch make a noise and turned his head. The handsome woman was locking up for the night. While still watching the door he said, "I'll tell you something, Marshal. That woman is one hell of a cook."

The tall man's gaze rested upon Ben. "Yes, she is. She's got the knack. They don't all have it, but Lizzie was born with it."

Ben cocked his head at the tall man. If he knew that much about the woman— "Your wife?" he said.

"No. My sister. I got to finish my round. Been nice talkin' to you."

Ben nodded his head and watched the tall man step into recessed doorways to rattle doors. Ben had been cautious in asking about the woman because of prior experience: almost every town he'd ever been in, the residents were interrelated and he had learned very young never to comment about some resident of a town, even after he'd been there for a considerable spell and thought he knew who was related to whom.

He watched a high, cold moon appear from a rip in some scudding clouds. Ben decided to get warm again and headed for the big saloon, which was an old log structure, part—in fact all that remained—of a smoky old trading post that at one time had been the only structure with squared log walls, a stone fireplace, a flameproof sod roof, and rifle loops within six hundred miles any way a man faced.

The place was about two-thirds full, bluish smoke clung like a cobweb when a man approached the bar. The iron stove was popping because the last man to feed it had pitched in a juniper burl.

The large swarthy man who stared at Ben had a bar rag draped from one shoulder, elegant red sleeve garters with white hearts embroidered on them, and an apron around his middle that hadn't been near a washtub in some weeks. He did not smile or speak, he just leaned there staring and waiting. Ben said, "Whiskey," watched the large man move away and sighed. The fat liveryman had evidently been right. That barman left the distinct impression that he would be someone to avoid if he got angry. Because first impressions are lasting ones, and also because Ben Moore had not come down in the last rain, his feeling about this barman was that he might not even have to be angry to be disagreeable.

But the whiskey went down smoothly and worked out some of the cold-induced stiffness, so Ben leaned there looking around, listening to snatches of conversation, sorting out the townsmen from the rangemen, and eyed an empty fourth chair where a session of stud poker was in progress. What decided him from going over there and buying in was physical tiredness, which had been more evident after his hot meal, as well as the fact that he had a hunch Lady Luck had probably not come five hundred miles south with him.

He had another jolt, paid up and returned to the roadway. Now there were no lights among the business establishments, except from the saloon behind him and down in front of the livery barn where a pair of old carriage lamps about head-high on each side of the front opening to the runway showed weakly through smoked-up glass mantles.

The wind had stopped. He looked up. The sky was starry, no more clouds. The moon, which was cradle-shaped, did not cast much more light than those dirty carriage lamps.

A heavy-duty top-buggy went southward behind a tired big bay horse. The man inside was barely distinguishable from the black upholstery and the black underside of the fringed top. Otherwise, there was no roadway traffic.

Ben crossed over and turned southward. His intention had been to get a room at the rooming house. There was no light showing up there so he walked in the direction of the livery barn. He'd burrowed into the hay of such places probably more times than he'd spent in rooming house beds up off the ground.

As he was turning toward the feeble light out front of the barn, a thick-bodied older man passed him with a nod. He was carrying a small leather satchel and had a big gold watch chain across his vest.

What made Ben categorize the burly older man as a physician was not the little satchel. It was the distinct scent of carbolic acid that lingered even after the burly man had trudged past.

Midway down the earthen runway another smoky lamp shed light. This time the lamp was suspended from overhead by a crooked length of wire.

Two men were having a desultory conversation inside the harness room as Ben went past on his way toward the loft ladder. He heard one of them say. "That's goin' to change things sure as hell."

The second voice, which Ben recognized as belonging to Henry Bullerman, added something. "I never thought he'd die. Charley Hearst's been here since I can remember. Like a tree or a rock or—."

"When it's time, it's time," stated the first man. "Doc looked wore down to a nubbin."

"He's not a young man."

Ben heard no more. He swarmed up the ladder, got into the pitch-dark loft and started burrowing.

CHAPTER 3

A Surprise

IN a town like Wileyville news not only traveled fast, it also spread far and wide. A man Ben Moore had never seen before in his life was eating breakfast at the handsome lady's café, and leaned toward Ben to gruffly say, "Too bad about old Charley. I've known him all my life." The man put a solemn gaze upon Ben and ruefully nodded his head as he also said, "And now there'll be changes."

Ben nodded and ate, wondering what the stranger had meant about changes. As Ben rose, he placed several silver coins beside the empty plate and returned to the plankwalk out front.

That was the second time someone had mentioned changes in the wake of the passing of someone named Charley Hearst. He shrugged it off and hiked down to the livery barn to saddle up and also to ask directions to that piece of land he had won.

The liveryman was not there but his day man was, and he said he knew the area. He took Ben our back across the alley, where they had an uninterrupted view of grassland cattle country all the way to the horizon, and pointed. "Maybe five, six miles. You can't miss it if you watch for two big cedar posts as big around as Mister Bullerman and maybe eight, nine feet high. That's the gateway, only there ain't no gate." The day man had to rush away; that thick-bodied older man carrying the satchel was standing in the middle of the runway bellowing like a bay steer for his rig.

It was a chilly morning. The sun was above the horizon but just barely, and for a half hour the buckskin horse's breath steamed. After the sun got higher there was no more steam but it was still cold. Ben had his old coat buttoned to the gullet, collar turned up, hat pulled down, roping gloves pulled snug, and because the cold made leather stiff he had to shift his shellbelt and holstered Colt several times before it either softened from body heat, or he became accustomed to its stiffness.

The air was clear. There were mountains northward and westerly, but those to the west were so distant that even with perfect visibility all Ben could make out about them was that they were over there, faintly in the background.

It was good stock country. Except for those northward mountains it seemed to flow like an ocean frozen in motion, sometimes flat, sometimes gently rolling with wide swales, all of it carpeted with grass: bunch grass, wheat grass that brushed the undersides of Ben's stirrups, rye grass, and lower, mostly hidden, alfilaria—called filaree—with its tiny lavender flowers and incredibly rich shoots and tendrils that spread over the ground making patches of darker green where it grew.

He watched for livestock and saw only one bunch of horses, no cattle. They were a mile or so to the north and he might not have been able to discern them against the darkly tim-bered backdrop mountains if the horses hadn't been moving. He assumed they were probably someone's loose stock, their remuda that had been turned out after being replaced by fresh horses caught and brought in for everyday use.

When he saw the cedar logs the day man had mentioned, he was still a fair distance away, but they were clearly visible because they were the only tall, dark objects in sight.

There was an old set of ruts that Ben had been following for about an hour before he saw the gateposts. By the time he was passing between them, the ruts seemed to aim directly for a place that appeared flat until Ben was closer, then spread out and became a very wide swale perhaps thirty acres across and about twice that in length, roughly from northwest to southeast.

Ben halted. There was a house down there, as well as a number of other buildings that were old, unkempt, badly weathered and warped, but solidly made. The house at one time possessed a single glass window facing the yard. The window was gone, probably taken to be used in another rancher's house. Glass windows were rare and very expensive.

There was a large barn made of big logs. It had sugar-pine shingles on the roof. There were two smaller buildings. One was the wellhouse, the other seemed to be a combination forge shop and storehouse. It was fully open along one wall and closed elsewhere.

Ben leaned on the saddle horn looking down there. He pulled in a shallow breath and let it out in a low, soft whistle. Hell, he had expected land, open land, not very good land at that. But obviously this had at one time been a cow outfit. A one-man setup like hundreds of others. Usually, depending on the cowman who founded these places, they either prospered and expanded with the years, or they remained as they were. This one had not grown.

He felt heat and unbuttoned his coat, removed the gloves and folded them behind his shellbelt. These things were done automatically because the longer he sat there in what originally had been mild astonishment, but which grew to become something close to awe or incredulity, the more he began to doubt that he could possibly be on the right piece of ground.

The deed gave surveyor's metes and bounds, which might as well have been Chinese writing to Ben Moore. He twisted to make certain those cedar posts were back there. They were. He finally patted the buckskin's thick neck and said, "Well, there's got to be something wrong, horse. All this place needs is a summer of fixin' and patchin', then for a man to get some cattle. . . . All the same, I expect I'd better ride to the county seat and get the deed recorded. Maybe someone over there can show me on a map exactly where the boundaries are, just in case I'm on the right piece of land."

The horse yanked the reins and lowered his head to browse among the tall stalks of wheat grass, eating the seed heads. Ben ignored this to shake his head. "I never in my life been lucky. But those are the posts back yonder, and there goes the old wagon ruts right down into the yard. . . . I'm about half afraid to believe this, but accordin' to what I know, horse, this has got to be it. Now tell me—what in hell was that old man thinkin' of to put his deed to this place in a poker pot?"

The buckskin chewed, eyed the buildings and shifted restlessly. Horses were not chairs. Sitting on their backs while they were standing still was hard on them, harder than being ridden.

Ben evened up the reins and squeezed the animal to get it down into the ranch yard. The horse was willing. He too was curious, but his curiosity was based on scents that got stronger the closer he got to the yard. Water, for instance.

Where Ben finally dismounted out front of the big old log barn, there was no tie rack, but at wide intervals along the barn's front wall someone had imbedded massively forged stud rings. Ben tied up at one of them, entered the barn moving slowly, went out the back where a set of rotting working corrals were, then circled around to return to the yard on his way to the residence.

He did not try the closed door, but stepped through the square hole where crowbar indentations showed how someone had carefully removed the window, probably without breaking the glass.

A wood rat as large as a house cat scuttled frantically toward the kitchen, making Ben's heart drum rapidly for several seconds. He had his six-gun out and rising before the rat dove into its shoulder-high conical nest made of whatever it had been able to carry or drag. Evidently the rat had lived in the kitchen a long time. His nest took up a third of the room.

There were six rooms, which surprised Ben. From the outside the house did not appear that large. There was very little left to indicate that people had once lived here. He found some pages from a child's book in the layers of twigs of the wood rat's nest. In one back bedroom where someone had made a bed frame of peeled saplings, he found the remains of a woman's black hat and one curled boot, as dry as dust.

Ben returned to the porch. The house smelled of rodents. Outside there was no particular odor, but there was something; he strolled back toward his horse, trying to define it. He halted near the horse and turned slowly back in the direction of the house.

The yard, the buildings, even the spreading land gave off a brooding loneliness, an emptiness. Ben led his horse out back to a stone trough, loosened the cinch, removed the bridle and leaned aside, looking around as the buckskin tanked up.

Eventually he looked down as he went to work rolling a smoke. There were shod-horse imprints in the wet soil by the trough. He finished rolling, lit up and raised his eyes to the farthest land, did not see a single building, and decided whoever had made those marks had probably been doing exactly what Ben was doing: watering his horse, and that probably meant there was a ranch somewhere out yonder. He trickled smoke about that too. In any country with feed for a horse's belly there would be cattle and cattlemen.

He inhaled, exhaled, stomped out the smoke, reset the bridle, snugged up the cinch before leading the buckskin back up through the yard to be mounted, and the horse abruptly flung up its head, small ears pointing, eyes dilated. Whatever was out there had the horse's full attention. He even ignored the growl of his rider and the sharp tug on the reins.

Ben turned slowly. For the past half hour he had felt uncomfortable, a little uneasy in this silent, brooding, abandoned place. It was not an unusual reaction; he had felt it before when he'd stumbled across abandoned shacks and cabins.

The sun was high so Ben took his time looking for whatever had upset his horse and saw nothing for a long time, until the horse bobbed its head several times and snorted.

A short distance from the rotting old pole corrals and the stone trough there appeared to be some kind of commotion out yonder in the tall grass. Ben could only see stalks moving. He looped the reins, yanked loose his tie-down over the six-gun, and started out there. The distance was about three hundred feet. By the time he reached the spot where he had seen the agitated grass heads, there was nothing there but pressed-flat grass, and a very dim trail, seemingly made by a four-legged critter who was being followed by another four-legged critter.

There *had* been something out there. Ben stood, thumbs hooked in his shellbelt, studying the imprints. Whatever had been there had been watching him, and it was not a raccoon or a possum, a coyote or a fox. It was neither a big cat nor a bear and aside from the fact that neither cougars nor bears foraged this far from timbered mountains, at least very rarely, the sign was wrong. The creature that had made those marks had larger feet in back than he had in the front. But grass and filaree made it difficult to make much sense from the tracks.

Ben raised his head to scan the westward country. Whatever those critters had been, they were heading in that direction. He was curious and interested, but none of this was really very important and it would be dusk before he got back to Wileyville if he wasted more time out here.

He made a short sashay past the place where the critters had been watching him from hiding, then turned back—and halted at the sight of a dead sage hen. He knelt, picked up the plump bird and found no blood. He turned the bird over, looked closer, and was about to toss the carcass away on the assumption that the bird had died of either a disease or natural causes when he felt a lump beneath some rumpled feathers.

Now his examination was detailed. What had killed the sage hen had been a blow by a rock. He found the rock. It was smooth and round. No animal Ben had every heard of used rocks to kill its prey—except a human.

He stood up holding the bird, walked back to his horse, left the bird in the barn on a shelf and rode back to the pressed-flat place where it was a simple matter to put his horse on the trail where those crawling creatures had gone westerly.

The horse did not object at all, as he would certainly have done if the animals he was following were large meat-eating predators.

The trail weaved although it did not materially depart from its due-west course. About a half-mile out, the trail went down the near side of a wide grassy swale. There was a stand of buckrush down there, not tall enough to be seen from either side of the swale but flourishing and dense nonetheless.

Ben drew rein. He had a clear view of the entire swale to its western edge and there was no sign of the trail going up there.

He considered the buckrush. It was not just the only place animals could hide, it was also the most logical place for them to have a den.

He urged the buckskin horse down into the swale while holding the six-gun in his lap as he rode, a finger inside the trigger guard, a thumb on the hammer.

Upon the western verge of the arroyo a ground owl who had been observing everything since the mounted man had appeared suddenly yielded to its fear and sprang into the air, beating with both wings to gain altitude as if fled northward.

Ben halted a few yards east of the buckrush to listen. There was not a sound. He stood in his stirrups to see over the brush, down behind it, but it was too tall so he eased back down.

With the gun held above saddle-fork, Ben went southward to go around the stand of thorny brush. He had little more than cleared the southernmost brush when he got a surprise. There were two mounds, side by side, with cairns of rocks at their heads that held aloft crude crosses made of buckrush limbs, which were never straight.

Graves.

They were not new and animals had been digging over there but someone had filled in the holes with more rocks. Ben looked away, up along the thicket.

His gaze was met by a very small man in an oversized coat, rolled up britches cinched around his middle with a cotton rope, and a hat whose broad brim had been whittled down unevenly so its wearer could see from beneath it. Behind the little man was a somewhat larger man in similar attire, but this taller one had both legs spread wide, his head down against the stock of an old Springfield trap-door cavalry carbine. He cocked the gun, making a noise that carried distinctly to the mounted man at whom the taller small man was aiming.

CHAPTER 4

The Tall and Short of It

BEN had been puzzled about the tracks he had been following, but what he was facing now supplied the answer to their uniqueness. Each of the small men had damp, muddy knees. Clearly, these were what had made the large imprints behind the smaller ones. Those two bizarre creatures, standing utterly silent and still as they watched him, had crawled on all fours from the place where the buckskin horse had first caught their scent to this place behind the stand of underbrush.

He loosened a little in the saddle as he spoke. "You don't need that gun. I'm not here to cause you trouble."

The Springfield did not waver.

"Well, mind if I get down?"

"Drop the gun first," an unsteady voice replied.

Ben tossed it ahead into the grass, then swung to the ground and stood at the head of his horse, controlling an urge to grin. "My name is Moore. Ben Moore."

"What are you doin' out here?"

"Looking over that old ranch back yonder."

"We saw you. We watched you go into the house and around the yard. What was you looking for?"

"Just lookin' is all. . . . Would you mind easing the hammer down on that carbine? At least point it in some other direction. Those old guns are almighty unpredictable."

The taller of the two short men muttered something and the shorter one came warily over to Ben, stopped and raised a grimy small face with very blue frightened eyes as he said, "My brother wants you to pull up your pants legs."

Ben regarded the speaker. He could see now that this was

24

not a small man, but a child eight or nine years old. Ben leaned and pulled up both trouser legs, then he smiled at the child. "See? No hideout gun an' no knife. All right?"

The child turned, calling shrilly to the other one. "It's all right, Jamie."

The answer came back brisk and businesslike. "No it ain't. Tell him to shed his coat."

Ben obeyed this time without waiting for the order to be relayed. Then he flapped his arms. "I told you—I'm not out to cause you any trouble."

The gun barrel wavered.

Ben looked at the small child looking steadily up at him. "My name is Ben Moore. What's your name?"

"Arthur."

"Arthur what?"

The older child grounded his Springfield and said, "Don't tell him nothing." He then walked closer, eyed Ben's six-gun in the grass but made no move toward it. He closely resembled the smaller child, but he seemed to be in his early teens, perhaps thirteen or fourteen years of age. He had the same very bright blue eyes and the same wavy dark-brown hair.

Ben eased down in the grass looking at them, and finally wagged his head. He'd heard of waifs, everyone had, but these were the first he'd ever come face to face with. He patted the ground. "Set, gents." Neither one of them obeyed. "Well, all right, stand up. Tell me something. Where are your folks? How long you been livin' out here by this brush patch?"

Arthur pointed a short arm in the direction of the graves. He seemed willing to speak but his mouth quivered and his eyes watered so he dropped the arm back to his side and twisted toward the taller boy. "Jamie . . . ?"

"It'll be all right, Arthur. But maybe we was wrong. Maybe he don't ride for Mister Hearst." Jamie scowled menacingly at Ben. "Do you?"

"Nope. I don't know anyone named Hearst. But in Wileyville I heard someone named Charley Hearst upped and died."

Both boys stared.

Ben patted the ground again. "How about settin' down and explaining to me what this is all about?"

"If you don't ride for Mister Hearst, who do you ride for?"

"No one, Jamie. I'm new in this country. Only been here a day or two. . . . Who was Mister Hearst?"

Arthur suddenly sank to the ground. In his man's coat and rolled-up trousers he looked more like a toadstool wearing clothing than a human being. He gazed steadily and unblinkingly at the horseman with what could have been the faintest flicker of hope.

Jamie did not sit but he sank to one knee holding the old carbine as though it were a staff. Arthur was very young; he yielded easily to what seemed to be threatening. Jamie was older. He also had a different disposition. It showed in the square set of his jaw, the suspicion in his eyes, and in his posture of spring-wound readiness.

Ben rolled and lit a quirley, trickled smoke and asked a question. "You fellers brothers?"

Arthur nodded.

Ben smiled. "Arthur and Jamie what?"

Jamie answered shortly. "Oakley." His eyes flickered toward the pair of mounds. "Our paw was young Fred Oakley. Our maw was Marybeth Oakley."

Ben punched out his smoke and regarded Jamie through an interval of silence before asking another question. "If your paw was young Fred Oakley, who was old Fred Oakley?"

"He was our grandpaw."

Ben pulled a grass stalk and chewed it for a moment before speaking again. "Did old Fred smoke a pipe?"

"Yes."

"An' was he not very talkative?"

"Yes. But not when we first come here and him an' paw put

up the buildings. It was after paw and maw got real sick that he stopped talking."

Ben spat out the stalk, raised his eyes to the edges of the swale, then back to the boys. "What happened to old Fred, Jamie?"

"He went away. After we had the burial he went back to the house with us, cooked supper and put us to bed. In the morning he was gone, along with his horse and gatherings. We was hoping you'd be him returning; that's why we snuck along in the tall grass to watch you."

Ben said, "Uh huh. Did he tell you he'd return?"

"He didn't say nothing. He hardly talked at all while our parents were sick, maybe a month. When they died he done just like I told you, he fed us supper, put us to bed and—"

"And we been waitin' for him," piped up Arthur. "I told Jamie he went to Wileyville for supplies."

Jamie's comment about that was given in a harsh voice. "That was last spring. He didn't figure on comin' back. I told you that, Arthur."

The small boy's mouth quivered, he looked very hard at the ground. Ben leaned to touch his shoulder and when the swimming blue eyes came up, Ben said, "You got a hideout in that thicket? Got any grub in there or anything to cook in? How about water?" Arthur's tears dried up but Ben allowed him no opportunity to answer as he shoved up to his feet, dusted off the seat of his britches and jerked his thumb in the direction of the buckskin horse. "You ride, Jamie and I'll walk. That sage hen one of you got with a rock will do for a start. I got a little grub in my saddlebags, but not much. I didn't know I'd be eating supper with anyone tonight. . . . Tell you one thing, we won't have to gather wood to fire up the cookstove. There's a wood rat nest in the kitchen taller than Jamie, so all we got to do is grab twigs and shove them into the firebox. You like horses, Arthur?"

"Yes, he likes 'em," stated Jamie, and watched Ben boost his brother into the saddle.

They started back slowly, talking as they went. Ben had questions. They boys answered them as well as they could but there seemed to be a lot they did not know. For example, they had no idea what their parents had died of and they did not recall the doctor from Wileyville ever coming out.

There were little things they innocently said that helped Ben put their puzzle into at least a kind of rough perspective. They had not come west in a wagon, they had ridden the steam cars two-thirds of the way, then had got outfitted at a town a hundred or so miles east and had driven to their land. Old Fred had already scouted it up and paid the railway company for it. Three sections, nineteen hundred and twenty acres.

They knew nothing of their grandmother, old Fred's wife, and they only vaguely remembered that they had originally lived in Ohio, had farmed there. It was the sale of the farm in Ohio that had financed their undertaking west of Wileyville.

By the time they were in the yard daylight was waning. Ben cared for his horse, slung saddlebags over his shoulder and trooped to the house. As they were stepping through the windowless front-wall opening he said, "Why did you leave here and go burrow into that thicket out yonder? Because you wanted to be close to the graves?"

Arthur looked up at his brother to answer, which he did much of the time. Eight-year-old Arthur was dependent on his older brother. Fortunately for them both spring and summer had been pleasant. But autumn was nearly past with winter close at hand, and even though it rarely snowed in the Wileyville countryside, it still got very cold and it also got very wet.

Jamie had been starting to help with the work before he was thirteen. He was on the way to adulthood, but what had happened had come very unexpectedly, very suddenly, and if Jamie hadn't had the kind of ramrod up his back he probably had been born with, neither he nor his brother would have survived this long hiding out and killing small animals with slingshots.

As he replied to Ben's question Jamie leaned the old carbine in a corner of the kitchen, behind the door. Then he looked straight at Ben. "We wanted to protect the graves. Varmints come to dig. We killed a few but mostly we run them off and chucked rocks into their dug places."

Ben faced the boy. "You could have lived here an' gone out there, Jamie."

"No, we couldn't have because Jess Hearst got our horses and once when we was comin' back from out yonder we saw him an' one of their riders prisin' the window out of the front of the house. We hid in the grass until they was gone."

Ben scowled. "Charley Hearst?"

"No, Jess. That's Charley's son. One time he told my paw someday he'd own this place."

"What about his paw, did you know him?"

"Yes. He was old, couldn't ride much any more so he went around on the range in a buggy. Sometimes a top-buggy, sometimes a buckboard. He brought me'n Arthur tow red wagons one Christmas and some heavy underwear from town."

Ben looked out where Arthur had falled asleep on the parlor floor. He did not have a bedroll. It would be cold tonight. Maybe by morning they would have fed the entire wood rat's nest into the cook stove. While still looking into the parlor he said, "How many horses did you have?"

"Six. A big pair of team horses, matched sorrels with flaxen manes an' tails. They was my paw's pride, for a fact. And four saddle animals."

"Maybe this Jess Hearst didn't take them, Jamie. Maybe they wandered off."

"Arthur and I saw him an' one of his riders round them up out back of the barn an' drive 'em hell for leather. They didn't know me'n Arthur was still here. I guess they figured

when old Fred left he took us with him—only he didn't. . . .
And there's something else."

Ben nodded and leaned to strike a fire in the wood box
after robbing the wood rat's nest of all the bone-dry kindling
he needed. As he straightened up he said, "What else,
Jamie?"

"He shot at us."

Ben dropped the dead match. "Shot at a couple of little
kids?"

"We was watchin' for them, but this time they was in the
yard before we could run out the back of the house. But we
run anyway, and they shot at us. Three times. They almost
hit Arthur because he can't run real fast."

"They were on horseback?"

"Yes."

"Well, then, why didn't they just run you down?"

Jamie pulled the kitchen door partway clear of the wall.
The old Springfield was in sight. "Because I shot back with
my grandpaw's old war gun."

The stove was loudly crackling. Except for the red glow
that seeped around the burner lids, the door to the woodbox
and a couple of other places, there was no light in the
kitchen. Ben cocked the firebox door open just enough to
have sufficient light to prepare their meal by.

He sent Jamie to the barn for his saddle blanket. They
covered Arthur with it. If they'd had a large blanket to put
over the window hole they could have kept the interior of
the house warm from the cook stove.

Ben gave the boys the sage hen and one of his tins of
sardines. He ate the other tin and wished he'd had some
coffee, or, better still, some coffee laced with popskull,
because this was one of the most unpleasant days he had
experienced in all the forty years of his life.

They slept on the floor in the kitchen where it was warm.
When cold roused Ben during the night he fed more of the
big nest into the fire box. They made it through until

morning without any real suffering. Ben had not slept on planking in a long time, but it was not much different from a bedroll atop caliche.

The boys scarcely moved after they had eaten and gone to sleep. By dawn light he sat up looking at them. It had been a devastating summer for them. Everything that should have happened over a period of years had happened all at once. Jamie'd had no alternative to becoming a man in the few months of just one summer. Arthur—well, Arthur was possibly too young to understand yet what a complete disaster had overtaken him and his brother.

Ben tiptoed out to the porch to have a smoke for breakfast. Last night they had eaten everything there was to eat. That posed a problem, but not an insurmountable one. He could ride to town, fill up his saddlebags, and ride back. He strolled down to the barn to look in on his horse. They regarded each other through weak predawn daylight, and Ben wagged his head at the horse.

"All right, old line-back, you heard them or smelled them or something yesterday, and now we got them. Now tell me something, you thousand-pound troublemaker: what do we do with them?"

The horse turned his big rump toward the man and dropped his head to lip around for something to eat. There was nothing so Ben took him out back and hobbled him. The horse hopped out where grass heads were so tall he barely had to bend his neck, and began the new day eating, something his owner watched with a sour look.

CHAPTER 5

Bits and Pieces

JAMIE and his brother stood in the yard watching Ben ride in the direction of Wileyville. Arthur sniffled and for once Jamie did not scold him for it. Jamie had a lump in his throat too, which he cured by loudly clearing his throat before saying, "He'll be back. He told us he would. An' he's right, we got nothin' to eat so someone had to go."

Arthur wanted to be reassured, but young though he was, he was beginning to learn something about having faith in folks and trusting them. Mostly, you couldn't—or if you could, you didn't know which ones. He felt for his brother's hand and clung to it, watching the distant horseman raise an arm as he broke over into a lope.

Ben had told them to stay out of sight until he got back, even though he was not convinced this Jess Hearst had done all the things Jamie'd said he'd done. In fact, Ben told the disinterested buckskin horse that little kids have big imaginations. He knew because he'd been that way as a youngster, and since those days he had seen the same characteristic in other children.

By the time he reached Wileyville the sun was high, people were busy. There was considerable wagon, buggy, and saddleback traffic in the roadway, and down at the livery barn where Ben left his horse, the fat proprietor, Henry Bullerman, turned from what he was doing and watched Ben Moore enter from out back and dismount.

Henry walked over. "You find the place all right?" he asked.

Ben was yanking the latigo loose as he replied. "Yeah. I think so. There's two big cedar posts and wagon ruts going

32

between them." Ben looped the latigo through the cinch ring and leaned to lift off the saddle as he looked at the fat man. Henry's mouth was open, his eyes were fixed on Moore, he seemed to be waiting for something.

Ben did not lift the saddle. "The buildings are old, haven't been kept up, but it wouldn't take long to get them back into shape."

The liveryman nodded. "Maybe. I ain't been out there in couple of years."

Ben continued to regard him. "But you knew those folks, eh?"

Henry's eyes jumped away. He licked his lips. "Nope, can't really say I did. By sight, now an' then when they'd be in town, but that's all. Never spoke to them."

Ben continued to lean, looking at the fat man for a moment before straightening back and jerking his thumb. "Take care of him," he said. "Bait of rolled barley, in a stall, some clean hay. I'll be back in an hour or so."

Ben walked up to the roadway pulling off his gloves. Once, he threw a look over his shoulder to watch Henry Bullerman grunting under his saddle, then he crossed the road and entered the handsome lady's café.

He was the only patron. As he sat down looking up and down the counter she arrived to take his order, expressionless and silent. He said, "Where is everybody?"

"Breakfast was over with almost two hours ago. Dinner won't be ready for another hour."

He nodded. "Well, whatever you have."

She departed. Ben rolled his eyes. Sometimes the Lord played mean tricks, like making that woman so downright beautiful she'd make a man's heart skip a beat just looking at her. Then he went and filled her veins with ice water.

The roadway door slammed open and slammed closed. Ben looked up as a very tall man sat down beside him and yelled for coffee, then met Ben's gaze. "Nice day," he said.

Ben had to agree with that. It was a beautiful day—for late autumn. "Mighty nice, Marshal."

"By the way, my name is Tom Calahan. My paw spelt it with two l's but you only pronounce one anyway, so Lizzie and I dropped one of 'em."

Ben considered this piece of trivia as Elizabeth Calahan brought two cups of hot coffee and then returned with Ben's breakfast. When she put the plate in front of him he looked up at her, met the big, liquid black eyes from a distance of about two feet, and said, "You're a fine cook. I told your brother that last night. I don't deal in flattery. You really are."

Her eyes widened, and she glanced at her brother, who was drinking his coffee and ignoring them. The she straightened up, said, "Thank you," and walked back to her curtained-off cooking area.

Marshal Calahan put his cup down, gently. "She appreciated that, Mister Moore. I know she didn't seem like she did, but she did."

Ben ate like a wolf, without looking up, without showing interest in anything but what he was doing.

The marshal let the conversation die. From time to time he turned to watch Ben scoffing up everything on his platter. He finally leaned back, wagging his head. "I think you got worms," he said good-naturedly. "Or else you been without for a long while."

Ben considered the empty plate and reached for his coffee cup. Marshal Calahan seemed to be a friendly man, which was not exactly a commonplace characteristic among the lawmen Moore had known. He said to Calahan, "You just happened to come in here—too late for breakfast an' too early for dinner?"

"No," replied the marshal, gazing at a calendar above the pie table behind the counter. "No. I saw you heading over here." Tom Calahan's very dark eyes came around slowly. "You know how it is in cow towns, Mister Moore."

Ben gave Calahan a wry glance as he nodded and raised the cofffee cup. "Yeah. If you don't ride out the same day you ride in, they're goin' to go to work on you."

"Yeah."

Ben drained the cup and put it aside as he twisted to face the tall man. "What's on your mind, Marshal?"

"I understand you got a deed to some land west of here."

That damned old granny of a liveryman! Ben hadn't shown the paper to anyone else. "You want to see it?" he asked, and Tom Calahan nodded. Ben fished out the paper, spread it in front of the lawman, then watched the handsome woman come back to refill their cups.

After Calahan read it, he folded the paper carefully and handed it back. Eying Ben thoughtfully, he said, "That's where you went yesterday?"

"Yeah. And spent the night. You know that place, Marshal?"

"Yes."

"Would you want to talk about the folks who died out there?"

"They just upped and died, Mister Moore. Doc Pittinger called it some kind of fever."

"How many were there, Marshal?"

"That died? Two."

"No, how many people lived out there?"

"Oh. Well, the Oakley's, Marybeth and Fred. There was an older feller, I think he was Fred's paw. Maybe he was a widower, I seem to recollect having heard that. And two children, both boys."

"What happened to the old man and children after the man and his wife died?"

"Well, as far as anyone around town knows, the old man took the little boys with him and rode away. Never been seen since. Just upped and abandoned the ranch. Mister Moore, I've heard of death affecting people that way. Sort of turned their minds numb."

Elizabeth returned to fill the cups again but Ben arose, shaking his head. He did not smile and neither did she. Her brother also arose. The marshal said, "Mister Moore, I'd like to know something. Do you figure to go live out there?"

Ben looked from one Calahan to the other before replying. "I don't know. It's good ground. The buildings need some fixing up. It's something to think about. I haven't been in one place more than a year since I was sixteen. The idea don' really hold a lot of appeal for me, Marshal—but right now I just don't know."

"Did you buy that land, Mister Moore?"

"Nope. Won it in a poker game up north at a town called Haverhill."

"From a gambler?"

"From an old man who never said ten words, puffed on a little pipe and tossed in the piece of paper to cover a raise. He lost."

Marshal Calahan was gazing downward. When his head came up he and his sister exchanged a look, then the marshal said, "There's a cow outfit a few miles northwest of that old ranch. A man named Charley Hearst owned it. He died a few days ago. He had a son named Jess. . . . Jess and those Oakley's never got along."

"Marshal, I been on the range most of my life. I've seen my share of bad blood over land, grazin' rights and whatnot, an' right now I'm getting a feelin' that you're worrying about something."

Both the Calahans were looking at Ben Moore, expressionless but studying him. Ben smiled and said, "I can get along with just about anyone, if they'll let me."

Neither of the Calahans spoke, perhaps because three big noisy teamsters entered the café, clamoring to be fed. Elizabeth walked away. Her brother nodded without saying anything more and walked out of the café. By the time Ben had paid for his meal and had walked out front, he saw the marshal stepping up onto the opposite plankwalk in front of the jailhouse office.

He went down to Bulow's emporium to buy supplies, mindful that his fat stack of greenbacks was diminishing fast and so far he hadn't accomplished anything more than ride out to his land. Whatever he decided to do, he had to decide very soon. If he remained in the Wileyville country, he would need a job—and because this was the wrong time of year to get a riding job, the alternative was to dung out the livery barn, maybe swamp for the saloon owner, or maybe hire out to the blacksmith.

He made his purchases, went down to get his horse, loaded the saddlebags at the store counter and was lashing them behind the cantle, ready to leave town, when the thick-bodied older man Ben recognized as the local physician came along. Ben stepped back to the sidewalk and said, "Morning. You'll be Doctor Pittinger?"

The burly man halted, nodded and eyed Ben. "Yes. You got a complaint?"

"No. My name is Ben Moore. I own the old Oakley place."

Alfred Pittinger's hooded eyes widened.

"I'm curious about what those folks died of out there."

The older man took his time replying. "You're worried the place may be contaminated, is that it, Mister Moore?"

"Maybe. Something like that."

"They died of a fever. One of the quickest acting, most virulent kinds I ever saw. Carried them both off in about ten days."

After Doctor Pittinger walked into the store, Ben watched him briefly before turning back to the buckskin horse. He left Wileyville riding west. The sun was on its downside but there was a lot of daylight left and he only had to go about five miles anyway.

The boys would be waiting, most likely as hungry as wolves. Ben looped the reins, built and lit a smoke, ran a casual glance out over the countryside, then picked up the reins and said, "Horse, those kids was out there all summer an' no one in Wileyville knew it. I suppose that's possible, them hiding an' sneakin' around like coyotes. But it sticks in my craw that this Jess Hearst feller who knew they were somewhere out there didn't make a real effort to find them. If for no other reason than to ship them out of the country. . . . And that long-legged marshal—I got the feelin' he wasn't being real open with me. . . . I think we got to make up our minds, Buckskin: either ride away and find us a job that'll keep us goin' until next summer, or stay here. An' I got a hunch that if we stay here, we're likely to regret it for the rest of our lives. What do you think?"

The buckskin, accustomed to these monologues, walked steadily along without even tipping his ears back. He walked like that on slack reins right down into the yard of the old ranch and stopped in front of the barn near the stud rings.

Ben tied him, took down the saddlebags, crossed to the house and dumped them on the kitchen table, then went through the dingy building looking for Jamie and his brother.

They were not in the house. He went down to the barn to take care of his horse and looked for them inside and outside the barn.

He finally stood in the center of the yard with cupped hands and called their names. The only replies he got back were echoes of his own voice.

He blew out a deep breath. Since they had been hungry when he left, he hoped they had simply gone hunting with their slingshots.

They hadn't.

CHAPTER 6

A Night to Remember

THERE was not a lot of daylight left. Perhaps a couple of hours. Probably not enough to help him cover the distance to the swale.

Of course if they were hunting, they might continue to do so right up until dusk. He had told them he would return as soon as he could. If they had not seen him return to the yard, they would have no particular reason to cut short the hunting expedition.

He would give them until sundown. Meanwhile he emptied the saddlebags and lashed them back on his saddle, turned out and hobbled the buckskin and searched among the out buildings for something he could nail over the window hole.

When dusk arrived and the lads had not returned, he alternately worried and swore. Later, with full night down and no sign of them, he made a skimpy meal for himself because he was not particularly hungry.

He'd bought candles so he lighted two of them in the kitchen. A man did not do his best thinking when he was worried, but as Ben rolled a smoke, it occurred to him that now would be a very good time to decide whether he was going to fish or cut bait.

An hour later he left the kitchen to restlessly stroll the yard. He even walked out a short distance where the buckskin horse was standing in a hip-shot drowse, as full as a tick. The horse opened one eye as his owner walked up, then the other eye, considering Ben with neither apprehension nor fondness. When the man rolled a cigarette the horse narrowed its eyes against the match flare and shifted stance slightly.

Ben listened to the great depth of night silence, then casually turned in the direction of the house, where puny candlelight shone weakly through the front wall where the window had been. Suddenly, something large and bulky abruptly moved in front of that sickly light and kept on moving until it was beyond the window.

Ben dropped the smoke and ground it underfoot and regretted lighting the thing in the first place because that match flare was a dead giveaway, if whoever that was had happened to be looking out behind the barn when he lit up. But he assumed the person had not been looking toward the barn, otherwise the intruder would not have stalked the house. It did not occur to him that he might *not* be the object of the stalker's interest.

Hair rose along the back of Ben's neck. He really had not got a good look at the apparition. He had been too surprised at seeing it, and it had been moving swiftly from the left side of the house toward the right side.

It had to have been a man because a bear—or any other large animal he could imagine—would not stalk inside can-dlelit houses on dark nights.

The horse hopped and Ben turned. Something was out there that worried the buckskin. A sudden hunch gripped Ben for seconds, then he very slowly glided downward in the grass, reached back to yank loose the holster tie-down and with his back to the house, intently watched the buckskin.

The horse had picked up a scent. It was too dark for it to have seen anything. He knew his horse—whatever was out there was not a meat-eating predator, or the horse would be hopping madly to escape it.

It was a man. Ben was convinced of that before a lean silhouette came into sight from the northwest, talking softly and quietly as he approached the horse.

Ben sank lower and put his hat aside. The man was still approaching, making reassuring sounds. He had not frightened the horse. It seemed very curious about the stranger but not afraid of him.

When the man got close enough to gently place a hand on the horse's neck, he said, "Now, you just stand still, partner, an' I'll take off them hobbles an' you'll be as free as the wind. Go anywhere you want to. Long way off."

The man eased downward with his hand sliding down the horse's body, down his leg, and stopped moving when it found the hobbles.

Ben came up to his full height soundlessly. The stranger was groping for the buckles to free the horse when Ben raised his Colt and cocked it.

The silhouette jumped up, then seemed to freeze. After a moment he raised his head. Ben walked toward him, went around the man on the right side, lifted out his six-gun and hurled it backhand with considerable force, then he leaned and pushed the barrel of his handgun to within six inches of the stranger's face and said, "What is your name?"

The cowboy's eyes were bulging as he stared at the gun barrel. "Pete Bruno."

"Sit flat down, Pete. Good. Now keep your hands in your lap and keep your voice down. You understand?"

"Yes." Pete Bruno finally rolled up his eyes to the face of the stocky man leaning above him.

"Pete, who is over at the house?"

". . . The house . . . ?"

"I'm goin' to blow your head off."

". . . Jess."

"What's he up to?"

"Lookin' for you."

"Then what?"

Pete Bruno swallowed and blinked. "I don't know. But he don't want you here."

"How did he know I was out here?"

"We heard yestiddy there was a rider nosin' around out here. I kept watch today and seen you ride in."

"Why don't he want me here?"

"Because this place belongs to him."

Ben squatted, still holding the cocked gun up, and aimed. "Is that what he told you?"

"Yeah. Told us all he got a quit claim from the old man who was left after them other folks died."

"And the little boys?"

Pete Bruno's eyes wandered away. "What little boys?"

Ben eased down the gun hammer, holstered the weapon, tugged on his roping gloves and did all of it without taking his eyes off the unarmed cowboy. He was very fast. And it was also very dark. The cowboy did not see the hand coming until it connected and bowled him backward. When he struggled back into a sitting position Ben Moore was standing. He gestured. "Get up, Pete."

Bruno obeyed, but he came up after balancing with one hand against the ground while he looked up. He sprang sideways, like a crab.

Ben fell on him, drove his face through the grass into the ground, lifted his head by the hair and slammed his face down, hard. The Ben shoved off and stood up, waiting.

Pete Bruno fumbled around on the ground. His nose was bleeding. Ben caught him by the shoulder and wrenched him upright. He said, "Once more, Pete: what about the little boys? . . . You hang fire again and I'm going to bust your head with my gun barrel. *What about the little boys?!*"

Bruno leaned to let blood drip. "They . . . we tried to catch them. Come close once but the biggest one had an old rifle and shot at us. Jess said t'hell with them. They'll starve this winter."

Ben eyed the battered rider. "He shot at you?"

"Yeah."

"After you shot at him!"

Bruno made a weak cough and expectorated, otherwise he was silent.

So it hadn't been Jamie's imagination that they had shot at

Jamie and his brother. Ben put a hand on Bruno and said, "Face down in the grass."

He used the cowboy's two belts to lash his arms in back and bind his legs at the ankles. For a gag he had to tear a sleeve from Bruno's shirt because the man had no bandana or handkerchief. Before arising he warned Bruno about trying to work free or making a noise.

The buckskin horse had hopped a yard or two away during the scuffle in the grass and was now watching everything, wide awake and interested. When Ben walked in the direction of the barn the horse's interest was still on the man bellydown in the grass.

From the dark interior of the barn it was possible to see the front of the house. Ben stood a long time up near the front opening. By now Jess Hearst had probably got inside the house and found it empty. He was speculating about what Hearst would do next when a steel horseshoe struck stone on the east side of the yard near the combination shoeing shed and storehouse.

He could not walk directly over there across the yard, and by the time he could get around the yard at its north end and begin walking down in the direction of the outbuilding, Hearst would no longer be there.

He remained in the barn and waited. Hearst would eventually come looking for his rider. It was a good guess. The second time he heard a steel shoe over granite it was north of the yard out where neither starlight nor weak moonlight made visibility adequate to see even moving objects, but when he returned to the rear barn opening he saw them. Two horses, one being ridden, one being led. The rider was reining out where the buckskin horse was still standing and now he was fairly close.

Ben considered his chances of getting out there before he was seen. He had to move fast, otherwise the rider was going to find Pete Bruno.

This time Ben's chances of surprising someone were a lot

less than they had been earlier. There was no way to reach Bruno without being a target every foot of the way. He swore under his breath, held the six-gun at his side and started walking.

The mounted man saw Moore's hobbled animal and stopped in his tracks. He did not see Moore, who was slightly behind him and to one side.

A sharp voice called softly. "Pete?"

As far back as Ben was, he could hear the muffled loud groan as Bruno tried to answer.

The horseman swung to the ground, dropped his reins and went swiftly through the grass to kneel beside his companion. Ben was still about sixty feet distant. He could not possibly get any closer before being seen, so he raised the gun and said, "Hold it right where you are!" and kept walking.

The dismounted man was looking up, watching Ben approach. He face was a pale blur but there was enough backgrounding starlight for Ben to see that he was indeed a large man, and a heavily built one too.

Pete Bruno was threshing in the grass, writhing like a snake in an attempt to sit up. He stared at Ben from blood-shot eyes. His nose was no longer bleeding but it was two-thirds the size of a potato and discolored, but that did not show in the gloom.

He was still lashed.

Ben halted and wigwagged with his weapon for the kneeling large man to shed his six-gun, which the man did, then he came up to his feet very slowly, facing Ben, sunk-set eyes fixed in a hostile, dry, fierce stare.

"If you had any guts, mister, you'd have come in broad daylight," Ben said. He was still aiming the gun but had not cocked it, when the large man emitted a large grunt and launched himself through the air. Ben had no time to cock the gun before he was solidly hit by at least two hundred pounds of hurtling bone and muscle.

He tried to break the fall and lost the six-gun as he opened both hands to brace himself. The big man aimed a vicious kick that missed, then hurled himself downward as Ben was frantically stumbling away. The big man caught one ankle and clung to it as Ben tried to kick free. He was upended with the big man frantically seeking to at least get to his knees so that he could lunge ahead and fall on Ben.

Ben's lungs were pumping like bellows. He had been slightly stunned by his first fall, and also by the second one, but he got clear and kept clear as he looked for his gun. It was too dark, the grass was too tall, and when the big man was on his feet again he came after Ben with his mouth wide open. He let go with a roar that would have made a bear envious.

Ben was not large or heavy enough to stand toe to toe with his adversary. He tried to keep away and did fairly well at it until he came close to Pete Bruno in the grass. Ben's retreating steps ended when his heels accidentally struck Bruno. He fell over the cowboy and saw the big man sailing through the air above him—teeth bared, massive arms bent at the elbow, thick fingers crooked. He kicked against Bruno as hard as he could to get away.

He almost made it. The large man's left hand caught Ben's boot and closed around it like a vice. Ben rolled, aimed a kick at the other man's face and failed to connect, but the big man was wrenching and twisting so Ben could not get positioned for another kick. Then Ben jerked straight up off the ground from the waist, cocked his right fist high and fired it. The shock of direct contact was painful but the big man's leering, savage face was gone, as was his grip on Ben's boot.

Ben could not stand up. He sat there looking at the heavy mass of his unconscious adversary, then at Pete Bruno, who was staring in disbelief at the inert body close by.

Finally, by using both hands, he was able to get upright. His hands hurt, his legs, even his back and chest hurt.

Flexing both hands, he went out to retrieve his six-gun, dropped it into the holster and returned to stand looking down at Bruno, who stared back, huge nose beginning to squeeze the flesh up around his eyes.

Ben knelt, released the cowboy, helped him arise and pointed. "Is that Jess Hearst?"

Bruno nodded. When he spoke there was no enmity in his voice, but there was obvious shock. "Yeah . . . it wouldn't have happened in daylight. He never seen it coming in the dark."

Ben searched until he found their handguns, shoved them down the front of his britches and pointed out where two saddled horses were grazing with their reins dragging and said, "Let's see if you can chum your way up to those two."

Pete Bruno hesitated. "You goin' to do anything to Jess?"

Ben looked down. "I don't know. Pete, you got your pocket knife with you—the one with the castratin' blade?"

Bruno stiffened all over. "God! You wouldn't do a thing like that."

"You got your knife, Pete?"

"No," the cowboy lied loudly.

"Then I guess I won't. But you tell this overgrown bully for none of you to ever come onto my land again. Ever. If you do, partner, I won't alter you, I'll shoot you on sight, and I'm good at hiding and watching. . . . You think he'll listen?"

Bruno gingerly explored his huge purple nose. "I'll go get the horses," he said and walked away none too steadily.

Ben hunkered down beside the unconscious large man, studied his face, his hand-carved shellbelt and elegant Mexican boots, spat aside and gently rubbed the back of his head, which was beginning to ache. By morning he would have a horse-sized headache. He'd landed on the back of his head twice.

He exhaled a big, noisy breath, flopped Hearst onto his stomach and arose to wait until Bruno came back riding one and leading one.

The cowboy leaned from the saddle. "He ain't come round yet? I'll bet you killed him."

"In that case," stated Ben Moore dispassionately, "someone else won't have to do it. Get down and maybe between the two of us we can get him astride."

"He'll just fall off."

"Then you can drag him. Get hold. Now—lift!"

It was close, they almost were unable to get him up there, but while Bruno held on one side, Ben Moore got his shoulders under Hearst on the other side and raised up.

The cowman groaned and scrabbled around with bent fingers until he found the saddle leather.

Ben held him upright. "Pete, balance him. Don't let him fall an' he'll be all right directly." As Bruno moved up to balance his employer, Ben tapped his chest with a stiff finger. "Remember, partner, there's not goin' to be a next time. Not here on the Oakley place. I mean it, Pete, I'll drop the first one of you boys from the Hearst ranch I find over here."

CHAPTER 7

A New Worry

IN the morning Ben was looking for his horse through a thick layer of ground fog when a familiar voice that seemed to range between the sounds of childhood and an uneven bass of manhood suddenly spoke from behind him.

"Did you fetch some grub?"

Ben turned. The sun was still below the horizon but false dawn's sickly grayness helped visibility, so at least at close range, Ben saw them. The two were standing close together, the knee-deep fog giving them the appearance of ghosts.

His breath came out sharply. "Where in hell have you been?" he demanded.

"Hiding," Arthur said in his soft, piping childhood voice.

"Why?"

Jamie replied. "Because we seen a rider skulkin' out yonder couple hours after you left. He'd go out of sight, then reappear somewhere else. We left out the back way, kept the house between us an' him and went out a ways to hide in the grass."

Ben draped the catchrope from his shoulder and walked over to them. They were soggy wet from dew and fog. "Didn't you see the candles last night?"

"Yes, but we knew they was watchin' the yard. We knew you was in the house, but we was afraid to try and get back there."

Ben reset his hat. "You're soaked. Come along, we got to dry you out."

As he turned in the direction of the house Arthur piped up. "We been wet before. Did you bring something to eat?"

He slowed until one was on each side of him, then he smiled. "Yeah. I thought you had gone hunting."

Jamie fished something from a ragged coat pocket and mutely held it up. Ben took it, recognized it as a slingshot and wagged his head. One of the lengths of coarse black rubber was broken. He handed it back. They were hungry for a fact.

At the house, as he was feeding twigs from their diminishing supply of kindling from the wood rat's nest into the firebox, he told them of his encounter with Jess Hearst and his rider. They listened in awe, watching every move he made. Arthur finally said, "You whupped the two of them?" His regard of Ben Moore showed wide-eyed admiration. "Mister Hearst is big. Real big."

Ben mounded hot food on three spanking-new tin plates and motioned for them to eat. They required no urging. He also fed more wood into the stove to get the kitchen hot enough to dry their ragged clothing. Finally, he sat with them and ate, but they were finished before he was half through and they were obviously still hungry. He shared what remained of his breakfast with them, watched them go after it and sat back to roll a smoke.

One thing was clear—what he could carry in his saddlebags was not going to be enough. Whatever the boys had been existing on prior to his arrival had kept their bodies and souls together, but just barely. They were constantly hungry.

It was not just that his money was going to give out that bothered him. His encounter with Jess Hearst had left him with no doubt but that the moment Ben headed for Wileyville to fill his saddlebags again, Hearst would come after the boys. He wouldn't even wait for nightfall the next time. That would leave Arthur and Jamie at the mercy of a man who had already tried to shoot them once.

He stubbed out the smoke. He had not told them why he had appeared at the ranch, so he toyed with the idea of telling them now. The reason he had not done it was simple:

he did not want to tell them in plain words what he knew they suspected—that their grandfather had abandoned them.

They had been hanging onto a thin hope, otherwise he doubted that they would have remained near the ranch. He got up and went to stand by the window hole looking out where dawn light was brightening the world. He was furious with the old man. Not entirely because the old devil had abandoned his grandsons, but because he had tossed that damned deed to this land into the poker pot—which was the only reason Ben Moore was up to his hocks in serious trouble now.

Jamie came soundlessly up beside him and said, "That was good. A real breakfast."

Ben looked past. "Where's your brother?"

"He's asleep. I got him settled next to the stove where he'll stay warm. . . . He's got the sniffles."

Ben gazed at the older boy. "The sniffles?"

"Yes. He commenced havin' them a couple of days ago. He shivers now an' then, and don't seem able to be warm even when the sun is shining. Mister Moore?"

"What?"

"I don't know how to tell you how beholden we are to you."

Ben met the lad's direct, candid stare. After a moment he looked away and cleared his throat. If he'd had that old man from Haverhill in front of him right now, he'd shoot him. Eventually he sighed and said, "Jamie, I don't know what we're goin' to do, but I don't want to go back to town for more grub an' leave you fellers here. Not after last night."

"We could go over to our hideout, Mister Moore. They never found us there."

"Because they didn't try, Jamie. They could find you any time they set out to do it. Besides, hiding out over there isn't goin' to settle our problems."

Arthur coughed in the kitchen. Ben turned to listen. It

was a deep-down, wet cough. He and Jamie exchanged a look. Jamie said, "It'll clear up. He's tough."

Ben studied the grimy thin face with its resolute eyes and reached to roughly rest a hand on the boy's shoulder as he said, "Yeah, it'll clear up. . . . Jamie, winter's coming."

The lad said nothing. He was watching Ben's face. Out behind the barn the buckskin horse whinnied. Ben straightened up, told Jamie to stay with his brother and stepped through the window hole.

The horse might have made that noise because he wanted water. He might have made it because he had seen or scented something—a mounted man, for instance, or a whole riding crew of mounted men.

Ben reached the barn with long strides and went down through it as far as the rear opening. He could see his horse now that the fog had been burned off. It was warily sniffling noses with a rawboned gray mare who had once been dappled and whose dapples had faded with the passing years.

Ben stepped past the opening in order to be able to see in all directions. There were no other horses and there were no riders, or, if there were, he could not find them and he made a very real effort.

The buckskin was clearly delighted to have a friend and the gray mare was not horsing so she was perfectly willing to be his friend.

Ben went after his rope and walked out there. The mare whirled to flee, then halted as the buckskin nickered at her. She bobbed her head a couple of times and snorted as Ben's approach slowed to a shuffle as he quietly talked to her. His horse hopped closer. The mare watched this and walked back a short distance. Ben halted, hung an arm across the back of the buckskin and waited, still talking. Eventually, the mare returned, walked right up and Ben caught her. She made no attempt to pull free.

He removed the hobbles from his horse and led both

animals to the barn. When he entered Jamie was grinning at him. Ben did not smile back. "Where is your brother?"

"Still sleepin' beside the stove on the floor. He's all right."

"Jamie, I got a feelin' that your brother isn't all right. That's why I said for you to stay with him."

"I'll go back, Mister Moore. . . . That there is Eloise." Jamie walked over to the gray mare, put his head on her neck and hugged her. "She was my maw's horse."

Ben looked for a brand. There was none. Eloise would belong to anyone who could catch and keep her. He asked about her disposition and Jamie laughed, still hugging the mare. "Paw used to say she's gentler'n a milk cow."

"All right, Jamie. I'll tell you what we got to do. You an' your brother ride bareback on Eloise, I'll ride my horse, and we'll go over to Wileyville."

The boy's blue eyes widened. "We can't go over there. They don't know us. Besides, Paw used to say Wileyville's a stockman's town. They don't like folks like us."

"Your folks weren't homesteaders, Jamie."

"That don't make any difference, Mister Moore. We was newcomers, an' we owned land they'd been grazin' over for years. Old Mister Hearst told paw an' maw one time it was somethin' that went with the territory an' the only way newcomers ever overcome it was to stay—live and work here for a long time, until folks no longer thought of them as newcomers."

"Old Mister Hearst must have been a nice gent."

"He was. But he was old; his son gave the orders. He even ordered his paw."

"Jamie, we don't have a hell of a lot of choices. Arthur gettin' cold and wet last night on top of his sniffles isn't makin' things any easier."

"He'll be all right, Mister Moore. We can go back to the—."

"Jamie, listen to me. He *won't* be all right unless he's looked after. . . . They got a doctor in Wileyville."

Jamie breathed deeply as he regarded the older man. The

ruggedness of spirit that had kept Jamie going since his abandonment showed clearly on his face now. "You know about things like the sniffles, Mister Moore?" he asked.

"I know a little about the croup, Jamie, and lung fever because I've seen them many times." As Ben said this his expression noticeably changed, as did his voice when he spoke again. "Partner, you go mind your brother. Be sure he's warm. Stoke the stove. When I've figured out a way to bridle the gray mare I'll come over and we'll head out. Now scoot!"

Jamie did not utter another sound. As he went trooping back in the direction of the house, Ben watched from the front barn opening, then wagged his head. He had just made a discovery. Arguing didn't get a man anywhere with half-grown boys, but laying down the law seemed to work.

He turned to gaze at the gray mare. She gazed back. Making a bridle that would be adequate for a gentle horse was no particular problem, providing a man had a length of rope. Ben had his lead-shank from which he fashioned a looped rein to a squaw-bridle, fitted it, then left the mare standing while he rigged out the buckskin.

Before leaving the barn with the horses, he went to the center of the yard looking for movement. There did not seem to be any, so he returned for the horses and led them over to the house.

Jamie appeared at the door, leading his brother. He said, "We're ready. We filled our pockets with some of the grub. Is that all right?"

Ben was eyeing Arthur when he nodded his head. The youngster's face was flushed. He boosted them astraddle the gray mare, handed Jamie the rope rein and paused beside Arthur to wink at him. The child smiled back. Ben told him to hold fast to the back of his brother.

They were ready to leave when Arthur piped up. "Jamie, you forgot the gun."

The older boy shot Ben a look of embarrassment and

would have slid to the ground but Ben stopped him. "Never mind the gun for now. We'll get it when we come back."

They crossed out of the yard by way of the shoeing shed, riding eastward under a pleasantly hot autumn sun. Off to the northeast there were banks of huge white clouds with soiled edges looking motionless above the highest mountains. But the clouds were moving; Ben could taste the faintness of something that smelled like brimstone in the air. There was a storm coming.

He looked around several times. Arthur's high color was still there, so it had not been caused by the heat of the stove back at the ranch, and that was what had worried Ben the first time he'd noticed it.

But Arthur was in good spirits. No doubt his big breakfast had contributed. Otherwise, he did not seem to share his brother's apprehension of arriving in Wileyville.

They started up a small covey of prairie chickens and Arthur complained about their broken slingshot. Jamie barely glanced at the fat birds. He was looking far ahead, where it was now possible to make out a couple of windmills and some of the taller buildings of town.

Ben was interested in whether the boys had ever been to Wileyville before. They said they had, but had not been allowed to leave the wagon while their parents bought supplies and loaded them.

They knew no one there, but Jamie volunteered the information that during the illness of his parents, Doctor Pittinger had driven out twice in a heavy buggy. The first time he barely more than nodded at the children and their grandfather. The second time he brought them both small bags of horehound candy.

As Ben turned southward so as to enter town behind the livery barn, Arthur piped up about the candy, then laughed. Ben looked at him. The high color was now sweat-shiny, which could have been caused by the day's warmth, but Ben did not think so.

The fat liveryman was not around. His day man took their horses, eyed the children's filthy, cast-off adult clothing and said nothing. But his interest was obvious, Ben saw that as he turned back toward the alleyway and led the way northward in the direction of the doctor's house.

Arthur stopped at a wire-fenced hen run and hooked grimy fingers through the wire as he looked at the chickens and smiled. Jamie reached to irritably pull him away, and he looked upward smiling. "Remember the chickens we had?" he asked. Jamie shot Ben an embarrassed look as he replied, "Yeah, I remember them. The ones we didn't eat, the coyotes got. Come along, Arthur."

Ben had never been to Doctor Pittinger's house and was not sure which one it might be until he saw a big drowsing horse in the shafts of that heavy rig he had seen before. The horse was tied to an iron post just outside a fenced yard.

He herded Jamie and Arthur up through the gate to the back porch and rattled the door with his fist. The boys stood like stones staring at the door, faces pinched with apprehension.

CHAPTER 8
In Town

ALFRED Pittinger was one of those squarely constructed individuals who give an impression of solid strength. He had pale blue eyes behind rimless glasses, a shock of unruly gray hair that was white over his ears, and right at this moment, a mouth that was being held tightly closed as he motioned brusquely for Ben to be seated at his kitchen table while he filled two stoneware mugs with black coffee and brought them with him to the table. As he sat down and shoved one cup across toward Ben he said, "It's a shock, Mister Moore, and that's a blessed fact. I never went back out there after my last visit, but the talk around town was that the old man took the children with him when he quit the country."

He grimaced and raised the cup to taste his coffee, eyeing Ben over the rim until he lowered the cup and said, "I expect that like most little boys they don't get near soap and water unless they got a maw behind them. . . . They smell pretty foul, don't they?"

Ben knew Doctor Pittinger was making this conversation as a smokescreen to cover his surprise. The doctor was also measuring and gauging the stocky man opposite him. Instead of answering the doctor's question, Ben asked, "Are you sure Arthur's got lung fever?"

Pittinger clasped thick hands in front of him and leaned on the table as he replied. "Yes. But that's a term that covers just about everything a person can get wrong with their breathin' equipment. If you're thinkin' about tuberculosis— he don't have that. But he might have influenza."

Ben pushed his cup away. Influenza killed people by the hundreds. "You got medicine for it, Doctor?"

Pittinger looked sardonic. "Sure. There's maybe fifty med-

56

icines for it, Mister Moore. . . . I've been at my trade forty-five years. I've yet to see one that even helps very much."

Ben stared at the older man. "He's goin' to die?"

Pittinger was irritated. "No, damn it all, I didn't say that."

"Well, I've seen a lot of influenza graves, Doctor."

"Not as many as I have, cowboy. More coffee?"

"No thanks. What are his chances?"

"Well, maybe pretty fair—now. Out there he'd have died as sure as we're sitting here. He's got to be kept warm—all the time, night and day. And he's got to drink plenty of fluids and eat three times a day, if he'll do it. Beyond that, Mister Moore, we wait, let him sleep. His brother doesn't seem to have it."

Ben leaned back and gazed steadily at the medical practitioner. "My money's dwindlin' pretty fast," he announced and watched the pale blue eyes across from him.

Alfred Pittinger sat a moment in silence, then heaved a big sigh and spoke. "You want to hear a little anecdote, Mister Moore? I'm going to tell you anyway. When I went into this business everyone said I could retire when I was forty. I'm sixty-five years old. I have this house, a good rig, two fairly sound horses, one for pulling the rig, one for riding, and if I'd accept 'em, I'd have maybe fifty head of cattle, a yard full of chickens and hunting dogs. Summertimes I get more garden vegetables than a man could eat in five years, but I've always been a meat and potatoes man." Pittinger laughed. "I couldn't have retired at forty, and right now I don't see retirement up ahead anywhere in sight. . . . Your money is dwindling. Well, maybe you can get work in town, although I doubt it. I've yet to see a cowboy who was worth a damn at anything folks do in town except maybe blacksmithing, and most of 'em aren't very good at that. An' you got two little orphans."

The doctor arose, got the pot from the stove, refilled their cups, put the pot back atop its burner and returned to the table. As he eased down he said, "You could send them to a big city where they have orphanages and workhouses."

Ben shifted, ready to rise. "Not on your damned life."

"Wait a minute. Sit back and let me finish. All right, you're mothering them like an old hen. I guess I can do something for them too. Leave them here. You couldn't move Arthur anyway. Leave them here. Maybe in a few years when you get rich, you can come around and we'll talk about payment."

"You can't do your doctorin' and watch them too," Ben said.

Pittinger shrugged thick shoulders. "For now let's just worry about the youngest one. While I'm out on calls Jamie can look after him. I have some friends around town who can look in on them now and then."

Ben considered the refilled cup without touching it and launched into the story of how he happened to be here. When he had finished Doctor Pittinger nodded thoughtfully and said, "I knew the old man, their grandpaw. He was a quiet, inward feller, nice to talk to. Mister Moore, you can't guess how folks will react to catastrophic trouble. I don't believe I'd have done what he did, just up and turn my back on everything and keep riding until the horse gave out. But I don't know, maybe I would have. Right now you blame their grandpaw for everything. Mister Moore, I'm a lot older than you are. If I've learned anything, it's that the easiest thing is to blame people and the hardest thing is not to." Doctor Pittinger smiled. "Are you going back out to the Oakley place?"

"Doctor, when I saddled up this morning I didn't know where I was going, except to Wileyville, and right now I got no idea what I'll be doing—except for one thing. The next time Jess Hearst comes rutting for trouble he's not goin' to catch me off guard like he did last night."

"Yeah," Pittinger replied dryly. "About work, try Job Upton at the corralyard. He might need another yardman. It's just a guess."

Ben arose. "I'm obliged. I'd like to be around town at least until Arthur is able to go back to the ranch."

Pittinger also stood up. "I'd like to ask a question: are you going to keep the boys?"

Ben had to hang fire before answering because he had only vaguely considered this possibility. Right now, he could say that he was going to look out for them, but beyond that he had no idea what would happen. "I'd like to keep an eye out for them until Arthur is up and around again. At least until then. Beyond that, Doctor, *quién sabe?*"

When he left the house the sun was high, there was a noticeable sultriness to the day, the air was still and halfway between the mountains and the town there were banks of enormous white clouds.

He went down to the café and for the second time arrived at the in-between time for the proprietor. Lizzie Calahan brought him coffee, went out back to get his bowl of barley soup, and as she was putting it in front of him her black eyes raised to his face as she said, "Have you found a place for your children?"

He blinked at her. She almost smiled at his expression of astonishment and straightened up to say, "Moccasin telegraph, Mister Moore."

He dropped his eyes to the steaming, aromatic bowl. He was very hungry and hadn't realized it before. That damned liveryman again, or his confounded day man. Doctor Pittinger couldn't have told her.

He looked up. "The youngest one's sick. They're up at the doctor's place."

"This is a poor time to be dragging two children around the country, Mister Moore."

He felt color rising. "Ma'am, those aren't my children. They belonged to some folks named Oakley who . . . " He stopped, staring at her. She had both hands pressed to her lips, eyes wide and glassy. He started over. "I won that old ranch in a card game up north, came down to look it over, and found those boys livin' like wolves in a thornpin thicket. The little one's maybe got influenza. The doctor isn't sure, but he's sick."

She lowered her hands. "But they left the country with their grandfather."

"No, ma'am. Their grandfather saddled up and rode off, leaving them behind."

She moved back to lean against the pie table. "But that was a long time ago."

Ben shrugged and picked up his spoon. She watched him for a moment, then whirled, removing her apron as she moved quickly past the curtained-off area of her café.

Ben ate, drank coffee, emptied the bowl, and leaned to call for a refill. He got no response. He called again, then gave up, put a small silver coin beside the bowl and went out front to roll and light a smoke. As he was cupping his hands with the match, he saw the handsome woman emerge from the jailhouse. The tall town marshal was with her. They spoke briefly, then the woman struck out for the café and her brother hiked in the direction of Doctor Pittinger's house.

Ben dropped the match, exhaled, and when the handsome woman saw him she seemed momentarily to hesitate, as though she would change course, then she came on.

As she stepped up onto the plankwalk she said, "You didn't know the Oakleys?"

"No ma'am. Just the grandfather. Did you know them?"

She did. "Marybeth and I were close friends, Mister Moore." She looked past him at the café window. "I just can't imagine this happening." She brought her gaze to his face. "My brother's gone up to talk to them."

He thought about that as he dumped ash from the quirley. Jamie would tell Marshal Calahan about Ben's encounter last night. When he looked up she said, "If Arthur is ill, you can't take him back out there."

"Can't do that anyway, ma'am. There's a feller named

Hearst who shot at them and snuck around last night. We met out behind the barn a ways. He wasn't real friendly, so even if Arthur could go back . . . They are just two youngsters. All they have is a busted slingshot and an old trap-door Springfield rifle."

She got a faint frown line between her brows as she looked at him. "Jess Hearst? A large man with—?"

"Yes'm. Jess Hearst. If size means anything, I've got myself a real big enemy."

She said, "Would you like another cup of coffee, Mister Moore?"

He eyed her thoughtfully. Was she trying to keep him there until her brother came? Maybe he was attributing a deviousness to her she did not have, and since he did not really care, he followed her back into the café and watched her go after a fresh cup of coffee. He put out the smoke and felt beard stubble before she returned and put the cup in front of him.

"It's unbelievable," she said. "Only five or six miles from town and no one knew they were out there."

"Oh, someone knew, ma'am. Jess Hearst knew. He told a rider named Pete Bruno they'd starve to death this winter." Ben raised the coffee cup and his eyes came up with it.

She returned his gaze. "They're lucky you came along."

He did not comment. He sipped coffee without speculating on what would have happened if he hadn't come along. Nor did he speculate about the trouble he was up to his gullet in because he *had* come along.

"Mister Moore?"

"Yes'm."

". . . I can't get over it. I knew them all, but particularly Marybeth. She was so gentle and kind . . ." The handsome woman turned quickly to hide her face and walked away.

Ben finished the coffee, called his thanks and was opening the roadway door when Marshal Calahan appeared upon the door's far side. He stepped back until Ben was outside, then looked from expressionless black eyes at Moore. "That's a sick little boy," he said quietly.

Ben nodded.

Marshal Calahan jerked his head. "Walk over to the jail-house with me."

The marshal's office was dingy. There were only two small windows in the roadside wall, both heavily barred. The room had a faint odor of tobacco smoke, horse sweat, and stale air.

Ben sat in one of the three wired-together chairs and fished around for his makings. As he was rolling the smoke, the marshal said, "Boys exaggerate a lot. Big imaginations."

Ben folded the rice-straw paper, licked it, sealed it and popped it into his mouth before meeting the taller man's gaze. "If you mean about the fight behind the barn, I don't think he was exaggeratin' very much. Jess Hearst is big and solid and mean."

"But you whipped him."

Ben lighted up and blew smoke at the low ceiling. "No. I got in a lucky hit, otherwise he'd have pulled my arm off an' beat my head with it." Ben smiled slightly, crookedly. "Next time it ought to be interesting. I told his cowboy if I catch any of them over on the Oakley place, I'll shoot them on sight."

Tom Calahan let that pass. "I talked to Al Pittinger. He seemed to think you might have something in mind for the boys."

"No sir, I don't have. At least not until Arthur can travel, then maybe the three of us could go back to the ranch. . . . Except that I got to get work. What money I got won't last forever."

Calahan inclined his head without taking his eyes off Moore. "Al told me. On my way down here I cornered Job Upton, who's got the local stage and drayage business. He agreed to hire you on. They got a bunkhouse at the back of the yard where his two hostlers bunk, and where now an' then a driver or guard will put up."

Ben said, "I'm obliged to you, Marshal. That's a load of worry off my shoulders. I want to be around where I can sort of keep an eye on Jamie and Arthur."

"Are you a married man, Mister Moore?"

"Nope. Are you?"

"Widower."

"I'm sorry. I didn't have any call to ask that."

Calahan brushed the apology aside. "What Liz is wonderin' is if you plan on keepin' Marybeth's sons—or what?"

Ben smiled a little and got to his feet. "I better go up yonder and see about that job. . . . Marshal, I ride for a living. I drift a lot. Until now I did anyway, until I came down here and saw my land. But about the boys . . . too much has happened in too short a time for me to have made up my mind about all this, and right now I better go see about that job."

Tom Calahan watched the roadway door close after Moore, and sat a moment, lost in thought. Then he got up and strolled over to the café.

There were lots of diners along the counter, along with a ripple of conversation and the smell of tobacco smoke. His sister was as busy as a kitten in a box of shavings. Marshal Calahan returned to the roadway to lean against an upright and watch the afternoon mail stage slacken to a walk south of town, then proceed with rattling chain traces up the center of Main Street on its way to the corralyard.

CHAPTER 9

Acquaintances

JOB Upton was a bull-necked bearded individual who looked out at his imperfect world with wary eyes. He was in his fifties, married, and believed unyieldingly in hard work as a cure for almost everything. When he took Ben Moore out back into the corralyard where a hostler was unharnessing the horses, he introduced him to the hostler—a tobacco-chewing, turkey-necked older man named Denham who said little, missed nothing, and had a loose-jointed, rawboned build. Then Upton returned to his office, and the day man, watching him walk back, softly said, "Mister Moore, you'll get along fine with Job unless he catches you squirrelin' away a bottle, or settin' when you shouldn't be."

Ben helped haul the harness to the three-sided shed where there were long poles to slide it onto, then followed the lanky man back to care for the horses. As they worked, he said, "This is only the second or third time I've worked in town."

The older man nodded. "Yeah. I figured that when I seen you crossin' the yard. Range rider, I says to myself."

Ben turned as the day man closed the corral gate on the horses they had cuffed and turned in. "You don't sound like the idea appeals to you, Mister Denham."

"Slim. Call me Slim. . . . It ain't that the idea don't appeal, Mister Moore. I've worked with a few rangemen who were handy. Mostly, though, they aren't."

"I'll do my best," Ben said and followed Slim Denham to the harness shed where Slim had been cleaning and tallowing harness when that stagecoach pulled in. Slim got another wool rag, pointed to the tin of two parts tallow and one part beeswax and went to work with his back to Moore.

Ben was busy for an hour before Slim raised his head, stood perfectly still for a long moment, then tossed down his rag and jerked his head. "Freighter coming."

He was right, but the rig did not clear the bog double gates until Ben and Slim were waiting out there.

The driver came down stiffly from his high seat, spat, nodded impersonally to Ben, then wagged his head at Slim. "I got rained on, wind blowed sand in my face, sun came out a hunnert degrees, and damned wolves spooked the mules last night. Only thing missin' was In'ians. . . . Slim, I'm goin' to get me a job indoors somewhere."

Slim cocked his head as he was folding lines and shoving them through a hame ring. "What kind of job? By the way, this here is Ben Moore. Job just hired him on. Ben, this here is Jeff Hoffman. He drives. Sometimes stages but mostly freight wagons."

Hoffman gave Ben a cursory look, a hand clasp, then picked up his discussion with Slim where it had been interrupted. "Well, I was thinkin' maybe of clerkin' in a store. Like the emporium. Somethin' genteel, as they say. Be near a stove in winter and under a roof in summer."

Slim looked across the back of the large horse where Ben was working opposite him and winked. Then he said, "Jeff, if you're goin' to work in a store you can't smell like horses and worse all the time."

Hoffman spat again, eyed Slim briefly from beneath thick brows, then turned and went hiking in the direction of the front gate and the saloon opposite and southward a few doors.

Slim grinned. "Every time he returns from a haul, it's something. Last time he was goin' into the shoeing business. Before that he talked about buyin' a string of horses and strikin' out trading."

It took longer to care for the freight animals. The sun was slanting. But time passed handily because Slim barely finished one chore before he got Ben started on another one.

Slim was not a fast worker, but he was a steady one. Once, when they were up near the back-wall bunkhouse he left Ben dunging out horse stalls, disappeared inside the bunkhouse, and when he returned ten minutes later Ben had no difficulty catching the scent. Maybe Mister Upton did not allow whiskey in his corralyard, but there was some cached in the bunkhouse.

They went down near the front of the yard to pitch feed to some corraled animals. Slim had a pocket watch. He flipped open the front, eyed the spidery little hands, snapped the watch closed and said, "Evenin' stage'll be along. I usually go to supper about now so's I'll be back when it pulls in."

Ben nodded. "Go ahead, I can handle it."

Slim said, "Yeah. I know that. I only need three, four hours workin' with a man to know whether he can or not . . . I'll be back directly."

Ben watched the turkey-necked man strike out on a diagonal course across the wide roadway and smiled to himself, then turned to walk toward the rear of the big, square, palisaded yard. He was halfway when Alfred Pittinger hailed him from the gateway, where he had looked in while walking past.

They met about midway. Pittinger looked satisfied. "Glad you got a job," he said. "The older boy talks about you a lot. I expect he'd take it kindly if you'd go up and visit with him for a while this evening."

While the doctor had been speaking Ben had been watching him. He did not act like a man with a dying child in his house. That encouraged Ben sufficiently for him to ask about Arthur.

Doctor Pittinger was cautious. "He's having a time of it. But he's a soldier, does everything I tell him, and smiles at me. . . . A man could get fond of Arthur, Mister Moore."

"Ben, Doctor. Plain Ben will do just fine."

"All right. Right now I'd guess Arthur's nearing the peak

of his fever. He'll maybe have a bad one tonight. Jamie'll set with him. By morning if the fever breaks, fine. If it's worse . . ." Doctor Pittinger shrugged thick shoulders. Then he brightened a little. "Elizabeth gets hot beef broth down that lad just by smiling at him. Of course, if Elizabeth Calahan smiled at me . . . It's hell to be getting old, Ben. Well, I was just walking past and saw you in—"

"Doctor, you know the folks around here so I'd like to ask you a question."

"Shoot."

"What's wrong with that woman?"

Pittinger's eyes widened. "Wrong with her? You must be blind. She's prettier than that big painting behind the bar at Benour's saloon."

"She's downright unfriendly."

Again Pittinger stared, but this time he did not answer immediately and when he did he seemed to be choosing his words. "Elizabeth got fond of a right handsome man named Will Elliott. That was three years ago. Her brother might know the rest of it. All I know for a fact is that after she'd been keeping company with Elliott for a while, he upped and married a lady who used to deal cards at Benour's back room, and they left town together and neither of them ever came back. . . . I don't know that this made her unfriendly. She and I've always been good friends. Maybe she's a little barn-sour on men. I wouldn't blame her."

Doctor Pittinger slapped Ben lightly on the shoulder and started to turn away as he said, "Those lads would like to see you this evening. The way they talk, you're about all they got."

Ben went back to the bunkhouse to settle in. His saddle and outfit were down at the fat man's livery barn. He would fetch his saddlebags and blankets later. Right now he stoked up the wood stove, selected a vacant bunk on the east wall and returned to the yard to wash up at the stone trough. He was doing this when Slim Denham returned chewing on a toothpick.

Slim halted, chewed his toothpick and eyed Ben Moore with candid interest. When he spat out the toothpick he said, "I stopped for a nightcap at the saloon an' heard an interestin' story about you."

Ben dried off with his blue bandana as he faced the other man. He said nothing.

Slim sighed and glanced around. "That darned evening coach is late again."

Ben stuffed the damp bandana into a hip pocket and continued to gaze at Denham.

Slim made a rueful smile. "Y'know, I remember them Oakleys. The woman was pretty as a picture and twice as nice as she was pretty. Her husband seemed like a decent feller. The old man—I saw him a few times an' never seen him without he was suckin' on a little pipe. He never said ten words." Slim cocked his head slightly. "It's all over town about the old man abandonin' the little boys—and one's at Doc's place sick as a tanyard pup. An' you come along."

Ben glanced past at the sound of a heavy outfit approaching from the north. Slim heard it too and turned toward the gate. When the late stagecoach wheeled up into the yard Job Upton came from his office. The driver came down as his four passengers piled out, looked around, sprung their knees once or twice, then headed for the café.

Upton had hardly come up before the driver spoke, loudly and bitterly, as he tugged off smoke-tanned gauntlets, the badge of his profession. He was a short, bandy-legged graying man with a nose as large as a big mottled strawberry, but not quite as red.

"The leathers wore through on the off-side rear wheel an' I didn't know there was anythin' wrong until I smelled the heat from the axle." As the driver said this he glared at his employer. "Y'know, Job, when I hired on, you told me them leathers was replaced every two months."

Upton did not look pleased. It was Ben's impression that not many men used that tone of voice to him. But the bandy-legged man was just getting started. As he folded the gaunt-lets under his shellbelt he said, "Where I stopped there wasn't no rocks. Lucky for me the passengers was all men. We dragged some logs into the road and them gents prised up the rear end while I took off the wheel, then they let 'er down and one of 'em carved a new grease-retainer from his boot sole. We put 'er on, slathered some shavin' soap and butter from another feller's satchel, put the damned wheel back on and come down here real slow. . . . You owe that gent for a new boot sole and the other feller for his shavin' soap and his sandwich. An' for two bits I'd quit."

The driver glared and went stamping toward the gate without Upton saying a word until he was gone, then he looked at Slim with a black scowl.

Slim faced the rear of the coach, leaned to run a hand over the rear hub and straightened up as Upton said, "Well, what have you got to say for yourself?"

Slim wagged his head. "I greased this coach last week."

"But you didn't put in new leathers."

"No. I never put in new ones if the old ones look sound. Job, this is the first time in three years." Slim leaned on the stage, gazing at Upton. It did not appear to Ben Moore that Slim Denham was going to cringe any more than the bandy-legged man had.

Upton threw up his arms, turned and stamped all the way back to his office. As the door slammed, Slim grinned at Ben Moore. "It's too late today, but tomorrow between chores we got to pull that wheel and maybe even remove the axle. And Job's not going to like it if we got to do that because this here is our spare stage. If anything happens to the other two, we won't have anything to send out to replace them with." Slim spat, eyed Ben, then said, "That's all for today. Care to go over to the saloon for a drink?"

Ben declined. "There's something else I got to do, otherwise I'd join you."

"Yeah. Supper. Well, if you get the urge later, you know where I'll be."

Job Upton was working in his office by the light of a glowing desk lamp when Ben Moore crossed the road and turned southward. His first day as a corralyard hostler had been interesting.

At the café most of the supper trade had filled up and departed. The liveryman Henry Bullerman was eating, as was Joe Benour, the saloonman. They nodded at Ben and returned to their meal as Elizabeth came up for his order. He regarded her quizzically as he said, "Whatever is hot."

She nodded, expressionlessly, but did not walk away. She seemed to be studying him as she said, "Have you talked to Doctor Pittinger?"

He had. "Yes. He said Arthur's fever is heading up."

She knew that. "Someone should stay with him tonight, Mister Moore."

"Yes'm. I'll do it. There won't be much call for me to be at the corralyard until morning."

The craggy, big saloonman turned. "There is quite a story goin' around, cowboy. Tell me something. Did Jess Hearst really try to shoot those boys?"

Ben eyed the large, poker-faced man. "That's what they told me."

"And they fired back?"

"The older one did, yes."

"An' that old man who lived out there after the younger folks died, he just upped and rode away leaving those boys on their own?"

Ben nodded.

Benour raised sulphurous dark eyes to Elizabeth, then shoved aside his empty plate with a violent gesture and stood up to fish in a trouser pocket for coins. As he was doing this,

Henry Bullerman spoke. "It ain't the first time somethin' like that's happened, Joe."

Benour turned on him with a snarl. "What would you know about something like that, Henry? You don't look like you ever missed a meal in your life."

Bullerman wisely let the topic die. After Benour had left, though, the liveryman made a small smile and said, "I talked to a drummer a few years back who recognized Joe. They both grew up in the same town in Missouri. Joe's folks was killed by In'ians an' according to this peddler, Joe's two uncles hired him out drivin' cows behind an emigrant wagon for six dollars cash and got rid of him."

Ben reached for his coffee cup and did not speak until the fat man had departed. Elizabeth was leaning against her pie table across the counter from him, arms folded. He made a rueful small smile at her. "Mister Bullerman was right about one thing. It's not the first time somethin' like this has happened."

She relaxed and lowered her arms. "You need more coffee," she said and went after the pot. When she returned she made a suggestion. "I can stay with Arthur tonight. It might even be better that way. He knows me. Both the boys know me from when I used to go out once in a while and visit with their mother."

Doctor Pittinger had specifically mentioned that Jamie in particular wanted Ben to come to the house. He explained this and, without thinking how it might sound, made a suggestion of his own.

"We could both go up there. I expect they'd like that. If you want, I can wait until you close up."

She nodded without any hesitation. "I'm ready to lock up. I'll meet you out front in ten minutes."

Ben leaned on the same overhang upright he'd leaned on before and rolled a smoke while Elizabeth locked up from the inside of her café.

He hadn't eaten, but he wasn't very hungry anyway.

CHAPTER 10

The Longest Night

JAMIE admitted them. He said Doctor Pittinger had been called out on an emergency. Jamie's attention swung from the handsome woman to Ben, wavered between them briefly, then settled upon Ben as he said that his brother was wringing wet and Jamie was frightened because Arthur did not always make sense when he spoke.

Elizabeth left them in the parlor and closed the door to Arthur's room after herself. Jamie led Ben to the kitchen, where he had been eating supper. As Ben straddled a chair and dropped his hat beside it, Jamie filled a second plate from the stove without asking whether or not Ben had eaten. The boy placed it in front of Ben, then went around to his own place. As he sat down he said, "I'm scairt, Mister Moore."

Ben looked up from wolfing food down, saw the raw fear in Jamie's eyes and put down his knife and fork. "We all are, son. Doctor Pittinger said Arthur's sickness is goin' to peak tonight. We can take turns settin' beside his bed."

Jamie picked at his food. "He must have drunk two gallons of water today."

"That's good, Jamie." Ben sat gazing across the table. "I got an idea and I'd like to hear your reaction to it. . . . When Arthur's fit again, the three of us could go back to the ranch and fix things up. . . . An' maybe we could get a loan at the bank an' buy a few bred cows. Lord knows there's enough feed out there for a lot more'n we'd be able to buy. . . . Sort of set up in the ranching business. What do you think?"

Jamie stopped eating. His resolute features seemed to loosen slightly. He looked down quickly at his food. "That's what Paw was going to do. He even got a few cows." Jamie's

72

eyes came up quickly. "Mister Hearst won't let you do it. He run Paw's cattle off, and we had to ride for three days just to find them. Then he run off our horses. Mister Moore, he won't—"

"Jamie," Ben said quietly. "Getting set up is only part of my idea. The other part is that we'll settle up with Mister Hearst before we get the cattle."

Now the youth's color faded and his eyes got large. "He's got six full-time riders."

Ben hadn't known that, and it made an impression, but he had gone too far to show caution now so he replied gruffly, "We'll have to do some figuring about that, but if you an' Arthur like the idea, I think we'd ought to try it."

Jamie's eyes were full as he looked across the table. Whatever he might have said never came out because Elizabeth swept into the room holding an empty pitcher. She handed it to Jamie, who immediately arose and went out back to the pump to fill it. In his absence Elizabeth faced Ben with a frightened look. "He is wringing wet. I've toweled him off twice just since we've been here. Does Jamie know where Doctor Pittinger went?"

Ben arose. "He didn't say. Elizabeth, do you know much about high fevers?"

"No. Well, not very much."

Jamie appeared in the doorway with the full pitcher. Ben took it from him and told him and Elizabeth to find clean towels, as many as they could. Then he brushed past on his way to Arthur's room.

Elizabeth had not exaggerated. Arthur was not only burning up with fever, his eyes did not seem to focus, his breathing was bubbly, and although he occasionally spoke, his speech was incoherent. Ben's first impression as he stopped at bedside with the pitcher was that Arthur was not going to make it. He was so small, so thin from neglect, so terribly sick.

Elizabeth and Jamie tiptoed in. Ben took the towels from

them, told Elizabeth to peel back the blankets and remove the huge old nightshirt Arthur was wearing. He soaked the first towel with cold well water and began bathing the child. As he did this, he told them to soak the other towels. Each time a towel lost its chill he tossed it aside for them to soak in cold water again, then he used the next towel.

Whether he was gaining any ground, or even helping the child hold his own, Ben had no idea. But he had brought down fevers in horses this way and had heard people say they had done this for other people. He did not recall whether any of those people had survived and right at this moment did not think about that.

Elizabeth's face was sweat-shiny. There were dark circles under her eyes. Jamie ran from the room to refill the pitcher. They could hear him crying softly as he passed through the kitchen on his way out back.

Ben did not look at the handsome woman, and neither of them said a word. When Jamie returned, Elizabeth soaked the soggy warm towels with more cold water. The bedding was drenched and water made the floor slippery. Arthur's teeth chattered, his small thin body moved in jerks at first, but later the movements became slower, less coordinated and sluggish. Elizabeth looked desperately at Ben. He did not take his eyes off the child, and when the towels were beginning to feel warm he sent Jamie back to the well for more icewater.

He lost track of time, ignored the wet floor and the sodden bedding. Once, when Elizabeth's exhaustion made her drop a towel she was handing him, he looked up and said, "Hold onto them, damn it!"

Arthur stopped jerking. Even the sluggish movements ceased. He tried to cough weakly and choked, his face seeming to swell and get darker red. Ben rolled him onto his stomach and held his head over the side of the bed, lower than his body. With both hands, he gently rubbed the child's back, up high. Arthur coughed and fought for breath. His struggles were weaker each time he coughed.

Elizabeth straightened up, crying soundlessly as tears spilled down her face. Ben said, "Towels, damn it! Give me the cold towels!"

She and Jamie poured cold water over the towels and handed them to him, both of them staring at the frail, thin body from stricken eyes.

Ben waited until Arthur was able to partially fill his lungs and breathe for a few moments, then he pushed again and the child had another seizure of coughing. Afterward, although Ben could hear the breath making deeper sweeps into his lungs, Arthur hung in his hands, delirious and fading.

He said, "Elizabeth, find some whiskey."

She replied without taking her eyes off the child. "I don't know where it is."

"I said *find it.* Jamie, go with her. Bring back a cup with the bottle. *Move!*"

When he was alone with the child, Ben did something he had not done since he reached manhood. He prayed, long and heartfelt. Arthur was breathing better, but each breath he pulled in seemed to weaken him more. At times there were such long pauses between breaths that Ben's entire body got rigid. He used pressure again, from in back, but very gently and with a slow rhythmic cadence. That seemed to help the child breathe.

Elizabeth and Jamie returned. They had a cup and a nearly-empty bottle of rye whiskey. As Ben was telling Elizabeth to pour no more than a teaspoonful into the cup, someone's knocking on the roadway door sounded inordinately loud. Ben jerked his head toward Jamie. "Whoever it is tell them the doctor's not here, then come on back. We need more cold water."

Ben said to Elizabeth, "Come around on this side. We'll

roll him over and you can hold him halfway in a sittin'
position while I get this whiskey down him."

"Ben! Whiskey might be the worst thing we can—"

"Come around here, lift him and shut up. I know this may
not help, but what else can we do?"

She moved swiftly past the head of the bed to help Ben
ease the child over onto his back. As she put an arm behind
his back to raise him, she said, "Ben . . . ?"

"Just raise him up and hold him still."

She made no further attempt to speak. As she eased the
child up, Ben raised the cup, got Arthur's mouth open, then
hesitated just long enough to seek her eyes and say, "He's
going to cough. Maybe he'll even gag. As soon as I get this
down him, we'll turn him bellydown again and hang his head
over the side of the bed. Are you ready?"

She nodded woodenly.

Ben coaxed the contents of the cup into the child. Elizabeth's arm stiffened. Ben dropped the cup and raised both
hands to turn the child facedown again.

Arthur did not cough. He had swallowed the whiskey
without even choking. Ben and Elizabeth exchanged a look,
then she moved around until she was brushing against Ben
at hip and shoulder. She leaned and pushed her ear to the
child's chest.

Until she raised up, Ben was afraid to look at the child. If
he was dead . . .

From the doorway a startled voice said, "What the hell are
you doing?"

Neither Ben nor Marshal Calahan's sister looked around.
She leaned back so slowly Ben's heart sank. She was staring
at the flushed, sweaty face. He reached for her arm and
turned her toward him. "Elizabeth . . . ?"

"He's breathing, Ben, he's breathing. Feel him. He's not as
hot as he was." She turned slowly toward the doorway. Her
brother and Jamie were rooted there. The marshal stared at
the child and tiptoed closer to see him better. He raised an

open palm and held it within an inch of Arthur's nostrils and mouth, stood like that for so long Ben's choking fear returned, then the marshal lowered his hand and turned slowly.

"Where is Doc?"

Elizabeth did not answer. She moved close to the bed again, picked up the empty pitcher and held it toward Jamie. He obediently left the room, heading out back again to fill it at the wall.

The marshal tapped his sister's shoulder. "Where is Doc, Elizabeth?"

She answered without looking away from the bed. "Jamie said he was called away on an emergency."

Calahan nodded toward Arthur. "What is this—isn't this an emergency?"

She picked up a wet, small hand and held it between both her hands. "It—Arthur didn't get worse until a short while ago, after Doctor Pittinger was gone."

Ben moved to the opposite side of the bed and leaned to listen to Arthur's breathing. It was still bubbly but each inward pull of air seemed to be reaching deeper. He straightened up and put a hand on the child's forehead. "He's not as hot, Elizabeth."

"I tried to tell you that as I was lifting him. You told me to shut up."

Marshal Calahan went to the front-wall window, looked out and turned. "A little while ago, Liz? Look out there, it's close to dawn. How long has this been going on?"

His sister said nothing until she found a chair and sat down. Even then, when she spoke it was not to her brother. "Ben . . . he is so—thin."

Jamie moved to Ben's side, looking down at his brother. Ben put his arm around the boy's shoulder and said, "Is there another bed, Jamie? We got to move him out of this one, cover him an' keep him warm. Whatever else we do, we got to keep him warm."

The only other bed was in Doctor Pittinger's bedroom and Jamie was hesitant to go in there. But Ben carried Arthur in, got him snugly down under the blankets and brushed the child's soggy hair from his forehead. He looked up at Elizabeth. "I hope he's just sleeping. If that child is drunk, you're goin' to haunt me about it the rest of our lives."

She smiled and lay down next to the child to share body warmth. Ben herded her brother and Jamie out into the parlor, where he left them briefly to hunt for that nearly-empty bottle of rye whiskey and drain it before returning to the parlor.

The whiskey did not make him feel much different. He had been too exhausted for too long. As he sank into a chair Marhal Calahan opened the front door and Doctor Pittinger walked in clutching his black leather satchel. He stopped dead still. There was water standing in the doorway of the room where Arthur had been. Jamie and Ben Moore were soaked down the front of their clothing. At the phsycian's astonished look, Marshal Calahan said, "Liz is in your bedroom with the child, Doc."

Pittinger looked baffled. "What's she doing in there with—?"

"She's keeping him warm," the lawman replied. "They been all night using cold water on towels to bring down his fever. An' they did it. The rest of it, they can tell you. I just came along a little while ago because I saw the lights while I was on my rounds."

Doctor Pittinger put aside his satchel and walked over to look into the bedroom. He stood with his back to the parlor for a long while. When he finally turned he said, "Ben, what in the hell . . . ?"

"You told me at the corralyard tonight his fever would come to a head. It did, Doctor, about the time Elizabeth and I came up here to sit with him. After that—maybe tomorrow I'll tell you about the rest of it. Right now I can't even think straight."

Ben shoved up out of the chair and started toward the door.

Jamie rushed to him, threw both arms around Ben and clung to him. Ben met the gazes of the marshal and the doctor, reddened as he pried Jamie loose, and said, "Remember. As soon as Arthur's fit, we're goin' back and set ourselves up in the cattle business."

Jamie thrust his closed fist at Ben and opened his hand. There was a light tan arrowhead on his palm. "That's Arthur's good-luck piece. He found it out at the thicket. . . . It fell out of his hand while you and Miz Calahan was puttin' the cold water on him." Jamie's haggard face made a haunting smile. "It works. Don't it?"

Instead of replying, Ben picked up the arrowhead, turned it over, looked closely at it, then put it back on Jamie's palm. He said, "If Arthur's good-luck piece really did its work last night, then, Jamie, I got another idea. Now we got a name for our cattle outfit: the Arrowhead Cattle Company."

CHAPTER 11

The Storm

JUST short of high noon when Marshal Calahan and Doctor Pittinger were sitting in the jailhouse office, Ben Moore walked in looking as though he had been sleeping in his clothes, which he had. But he had scrubbed, shaved, and combed his hair. He nodded, sought a chair and sat down as he said, "What does it look like, Doctor—is he better or worse?"

Pittinger eyed the blocky man. "He was dry as sand this morning and hungry."

Calahan smiled at Ben, who smiled back. "I think that was the longest night of my life," he told them. "How is Miss Calahan?"

"Didn't open the café until about an hour ago," her brother stated. "There was some cussing among her regular customers." Calahan leaned and tossed something to Ben. "She said to give you this."

It was a small buckskin pouch, split-hide leather as soft as cotton. Ben loosened the pucker-string and upended it. A palmful of gold coins fell out. He stared for a long time before putting all the money back into the bag, snugging it closed and pitching it over atop the lawman's desk. "I don't want your sister's money, Marshal."

Calahan picked the pouch up, hefted it and tossed it down. "It's not her money. It belonged to Marybeth Oakley. When she was sick she gave it to Liz to keep for the boys. Marybeth knew she was dying. . . . Then the boys disappeared—at least everyone thought they did, so Liz has been keeping the pouch in case they ever came back to Wileyville."

Ben was briefly diverted as Doctor Pittinger cleared his

throat. "Tell her to keep it until the boys are older, then give it to them," he told Calahan.

"No," drawled the lawman, "she says you're to keep it for them. Something about the Arrowhead Cattle Company."

Ben arose. "I got to get up to the corralyard—if I haven't been fired for not showing up earlier."

Al Pittinger shook his head. "You're not fired. I stopped by the stage office earlier and told Job what you did last night."

"I better get up there anyway," stated Ben, heading for the door. Just before passing through he asked Doctor Pittinger what Arthur's chances were.

The thick-bodied man turned his head and looked upward. "You're the doctor. You brought him through the worst of it. If there are no complications, I'd say he'll be able to walk in a week and go back to the ranch within two weeks. But you've got to get some fat on the lad, Ben, he's as poor as a snake. That means he won't have much resistance to whatever else comes along for him to catch."

Ben left them and walked up the same side of the roadway to the corralyard where Slim Denham was backing a team onto a light dray wagon. He looked up, called a greeting, then concentrated on what he was doing.

Ben helped hitch the horses. That complaining freighter named Jeff Hoffman was leaning in shade, watching. His work did not begin until their work was finished, but he strolled over on Ben's side of the vehicle and said, "Over at the saloon this mornin' they're sayin' you're a good man to have around when the chips are down. They said you saved a little boy's life last night."

Ben twisted to look around at the freighter. "If that's what they're sayin' they got it half right. Elizabeth Calahan did as much as I did."

Hoffman nodded, spat, pulled on his gloves and went to the left side before climbing to the wagon seat. As he was evening up the lines he looked at Denham. "Slim, I bet you never worked with a genuine hero before, did you?"

Slim helped turn the outfit until the horses were facing the roadway, then he winked at the freighter as he said, "I got an idea about what you can do when you quit, Jeff. Start a real, honest-to-gawd newspaper in Wileyville. You could start off tellin' the story of how Ben Moore saved a little boy's life."

Hoffman was unimpressed. He talked up the horses, then turned and frowned at Slim. "By the time I'd get a printin' press and all to put out my first newspaper, a dozen different crises would have come and gone. No one'd recollect this one."

Slim said, "I would," but the wagon was rattling out of the yard so it's doubtful Hoffman heard him.

Job Upton appeared in the yard looking pleasant for a change. "Nice night's work," he told Ben, as Slim Denham was walking away. "Doc Pittinger come by this morning. Strange thing about those boys showing up. I don't believe anyone in town had any idea they was still in the country."

Moore had heard this so many times now it had begun to sound to him like a litany. He apologized for showing up late and Upton brushed that aside. "It don't matter, not when a man's doin' the Lord's work."

Ben squinted. No one had told him Job Upton was a religious man. He had nothing against religion, but it made him uncomfortable to have the Lord brought into a casual conversation. He glanced over where Slim was hoisting that bandy-legged man's stage and said, "I'd better get to work."

Upton also glanced up there and immediately became brisk. "Yeah. Well, I just wanted to say folks appreciate things like what you did. . . . I hope to hell that axle isn't ruined."

Ben nodded and went up where Slim was chucking wood blocks beneath the coach. Slim pointed to the makeshift grease-retainer. "Now that's what I call a real dedicated stage rider. Not many men'd whittle the sole off a boot like that."

Ben twisted off the counterclockwise big wheel burr,

pulled the wheel and gazed at the axle. "How did you get the leather off without pulling the wheel, Slim?"

"I didn't have to. The leather was cut through and dropped to the ground when I jacked the rig up. Hangin' like a thread, as they say." Slim stepped close, shoved his hat back and leaned to examine the axle. He ran a hand over it gently, did that several times, then used a rag to wipe it clean and made a closer inspection before stepping aside to say, "What do you think?"

Ben felt the axle, examined it and gave his opinion. "It's been hot. Maybe some of the temper was taken out of it, but it looks all right to me."

Slim nodded. "We better pull it and put in a new one."

That is what they did. It used up what little was left of the morning and made a dent in the afternoon as well before they were finished and went after some clean rags and a coal-oil bottle to wash grease off with. They were sweating because what they had done was hard work, but the sun was a misty orb in a setting of closing-in gray clouds, so while the day was warm it was not hot.

Slim studied the sky as he was drying his hands. "Rain comin' tonight," he opined, tossing the rag aside. He was almost correct. The first fat raindrops made dust puffs out in the roadway as Job Upton appeared out back again to ask about the crippled coach.

Slim explained what they had done and why they had done it. Upton pulled on his droopy dragoon moustache, looking at the ground. Eventually he shrugged. "Couldn't be helped," he told them. "But them axles cost six dollars each. . . . Well, I'm goin' home. See you in the morning."

As Upton cleared the front gate, Slim shot another look upward because now there were an increasing number of raindrops stirring the corralyard dust. "Late stage'll be muddy when it comes in. You want to go to supper first this time?"

"You go," Moore replied.

Slim smiled as he was moving toward the gate. "All right. See you later."

Ben watched him reach the gate and stop dead-still in his tracks as a group of horsemen walked their horses past, heading in the direction of the saloon. When they were no longer in Ben's sight Slim turned back looking grave. When he reached Ben he said, "Did you see them riders? That was Jess Hearst an' his entire crew. From the stories floatin' around, you'n him locked horns. I thought that maybe, if you didn't recognize them, I'd let you know. . . . Ben, I think if I was you, I'd go to bed early tonight."

Moore said nothing, but this time as Slim headed for the gateway he also strolled in that direction. When he got down there Slim was already across Main Street walking briskly in the direction of the café.

Ben counted the tethered horses outside Joe Benour's saloon. There were nine head, but seven of them were tied together some little distance away from the other pair of horses. Seven, that was exactly the number Jamie had given him as Jess Hearst's riders, including Hearst.

He had not recognized them partly because riders going down a town roadway were too common to be noticed and partly because Slim had been directly in his line of sight.

He decided that Slim Denham's advice was valid so he went back to the bunkhouse, stoked the stove and had a smoke while sitting on an old bench. His guess was that if Hearst did not already know about the Oakley boys being in town and that one of them was ill up at Doctor Pittinger's place, he would know it very soon.

Ben put out the smoke and went to the tiny overhang-shaded porch of the bunkhouse to sit in a chair breathing deeply of the scrubbed-clean evening air and to listen to the rainfall. It rattled over the bunkhouse roof like tiny stones. Because there was no wind it did not reach beneath the overhang where Ben was sitting.

He intended to go up to the Pittinger place as soon as he'd

had supper, which he guessed would take maybe three-quarters of an hour, including the length of time that would be required for Slim to come back and take over. That was plenty long for anyone—but for Jess Hearst in particular—to hear all he had to hear and see red. He might even hear one of the stories circulating around town that Ben Moore had beaten him in a hand fight.

According to Ben's opinion of Jess Hearst, even if it hadn't been raining cats and dogs, he would have a few drinks, then he would start hunting for Ben Moore.

Ben probably had about an hour to make a decision. He had no intention of hiding. On the other hand, even if he could catch young Hearst alone, the results this time might not be as satisfying as they had been at their earlier meeting.

Ben lifted out his old Colt, flipped open the gate, snapped it closed and swung the cylinder. Each chamber was full. He holstered the gun, then drew it again, continued to do that until he could not improve on the draw, then put up the gun and spat out into the soggy yard. It would help like hell to know how fast and accurate Jess Hearst was, even though Ben would willingly settle for a fight without guns. He stepped to the edge of the little porch. The sky was black and the rain was coming straight down. The best Ben could do was make out things twenty feet from the edge of the porch. He went back inside where heat hit him the moment he entered, turned down the stove damper and waggled the bunkhouse coffeepot before placing it atop the stove. It had little more than dregs, so he left it where it was.

It was not possible to hear noise outside the bunkhouse so he had no idea there was anyone out there until a set of knuckles made an urgent rattle against the door.

It was Marshal Calahan wearing a black poncho that glistened, as did his hat, which he tipped down to rid it of water before walking past as Ben held the door for him. He went directly to the stove and put his back to it as he eyed Moore.

Ben said, "There's no coffee."

Lanky, big-boned, and tall Marshal Calahan gazed thoughtfully at the other man. "Jess Hearst is in town," he said, speaking louder than he ordinarily did so that Ben could hear him above the storm.

Ben nodded. "Yeah. So I heard. What can I do about it?"

"Stay clear of him," the lawman answered promptly. "He's at the saloon. Him and his six riders."

"And he knows about the boys an' me."

"Be pretty hard for him not to. That's about all folks've had to talk about today." Calahan moved away from the stove where he had left a small puddle. He shed the poncho, eyed the empty coffeepot and said, "I never cared much for Jess. I liked his paw, who ran the biggest cow outfit in the territory, but Jess is different from his paw. The old man was likable and decent. For all his wealth and holdings, he always stopped to talk, always had a joke to tell. . . . Jess . . . well, I wasn't here when he was growing up, but from what I've heard, Jess was an only child. His maw died when he was little and his paw spoiled him rotten."

Ben went to empty burned grounds from the pot and chuck in two fistfuls of fresh coffee from a small cotton sack. He filled the pot and placed it atop the stove. "Won't be very long," he told Calahan. "His daddy might've spoiled Jess, Marshal, but those two little boys shouldn't have to suffer because of it. The Oakley boys not only lost their ma, but their paw too—and old Fred riding away abandoning them."

Marshal Calahan removed his hat and dropped it atop the bunkhouse table. When he faced Ben again he said, "All right. I understand what you're saying. But it don't have anything to do with why I came up here in the rain."

Ben thought differently. "Yeah, there's a connection. Arthur and Jamie and I are goin' out to the ranch, get as many cattle as we can buy and start up in business as the Arrowhead Cattle Company. . . . But this other thing's got to be taken care of first, because if it isn't settled, the Arrowhead

Cattle Company is never going to work. Marshal, just how fast would you say Jess Hearst is with his belt gun?"

Tall, black-eyed Marshal Calahan stood by the stove inhaling the aroma of boiling coffee and looking steadily at Ben Moore. When he finally spoke he did not answer the question, he made a statement. "Not here, Ben. There's not goin' to be anything like that. Not in my town an' not on the range if I can help it. . . . I don't know how fast he is. You know where the cups are? On that shelf behind you in back of the flour tin."

As Ben went after them, Marshal Calahan studied him. When he returned with the cups for Calahan to fill, Ben said, "Marshal, if I sign away my soul for a loan at the bank to launch the Arrowhead Cattle Company, I'd have to be an idiot not to realize exactly what'll happen if we start running Arrowhead cattle out there. The same thing that happened to the boys' paw. And we're not going to have any money to start over with if Jess Hearst hooraws what we buy out of the country." Ben smiled at the tall man. "Maybe not tonight, but there's got to be a meetin' and a settlement. . . . Did you know Hearst ran off the livestock after the Oakleys died? That was about all they left Arthur and Jamie."

"How do you know he ran them off?"

"The boys told me. The gray mare they rode to town was one of their animals, their mother's horse."

"Marked, is it?"

"No brand, Marshal."

"Any of the other animals marked?"

"I don't know."

Calahan lowered his cup. "No markings, Ben, no ownership. You know that as well as I do."

"Their paw was no greenhorn so he must have marked his cattle."

Calahan drank coffee before speaking again. "I got to tell you, Ben, I should have gone out there, but hell, like everyone else I figured after the folks died an' the old man pulled out, it was just another abandoned ranch." Calahan emptied the cup and put it aside. He was reaching for his poncho when he said, "I'm goin' to do some scouting around. You know what the Oakley brand was?"

"No."

"I'll find out." Marshal Calahan went to the door, then turned and said, "I'll help the boys, Ben, but you got to help me a little. Stay under cover tonight."

After the lawman had departed Ben refilled his cup at the stove and stood lost in thought until the increasing violence of the storm broke into his awareness. It was raining bucket-fuls. Wileyville seemed to be directly beneath the heart of the storm.

CHAPTER 12

Water!

SLIM Denham returned to the yard and alerted Ben to the impending arrival of the late-day coach. They both bundled up and went out into the yard and, exactly as Slim had prophesied, when the rig came into the yard it was soggy wet and muddy. The passengers, three men and a woman, left the yard hastening in the direction of the rooming house.

Slim's face shone with amusement. He spoke loudly as Ben bent down to release the tugs so Slim could lead the horses away to be freed of harness. "Hey," he called. "Did you ever notice that folks who use water every blessed day of their lives run like hell from gettin' wet by rain? I got a theory about that. If folks pour the water theirselves they like it, but if it comes down onto them from the sky they don't like it."

Ben had the last tug hooked to the harness and was motioning for Slim to lead the horses away, when he called back to Slim, "Did you visit the saloon?"

Slim guessed the thought behind the question and answered it, not the question. "They're over there cussin' the rain and lookin' cranky. Just as I was leavin' Marshal Calahan walked in. He didn't look real happy neither."

Slim led the team to a rack outside the harness shed. Stripping the animals did not take long. Afterward they took the horses to stalls along the back wall and were pitching feed to them when a thick, heavy silhouette in a rain-shiny black poncho came toward them out of the gloom. Slim straightened up and leaned on his pitchfork, all traces of his earlier humor erased.

It was Henry Bullerman, the fat liveryman. He moved ahead into the scant protection provided by a narrow overhang in front of the stalls and was tipping water off his hat as Ben and Slim joined him. He nodded to them and said, "Nice night for ducks, ain' it?"

No one answered. Bullerman dumped the soggy hat back atop his head and looked at Ben Moore. "Jess Hearst is over yonder at Benour's place."

Moore nodded. Bullerman was the third person to tell him that. Slim Denham was leaning on his hayfork when he said, "What's he doing?"

"Drinkin'. Him an' his full crew. No one is crowding them." Bullerman rearranged his black raincoat before continuing. "Calahan's over there, settin' back along the front wall watching them. Some men walked out. Joe Benour's got a sawed-off shotgun behind the bar on a shelf." Henry paused to shoot a squinty look down across the yard in the direction of the roadway. "I'm well into my fifties an' I been in lots of saloons when a man could cut the tension with a knife. That's how it is over there." Bullerman looked from Ben to Slim before continuing. "This is a hell of a night for trouble, gents."

Slim nodded and turned aside to expectorate. Like most of the townsmen he both liked and respected Marshal Calahan, and did not particularly like Jess Hearst. "Big odds," Slim stated. "Seems to me, from what I know about Jess Hearst, he don't start anything unless there are big odds—in his favor. . . . Henry, how many fellers are over there, not countin' Jess and his crew?"

Bullerman pursed his lips before replying. "Maybe four, five . . . not the ones you're thinkin' of, Slim."

Slim thought that over while still leaning on his hayfork. "Well, you think it might be time for the two of us to circulate aroun' town and roust out the others?"

The fat man nodded gravely. "That's why I come over here. Is Jeff Hoffman in town?"

"No. He's gone on a run. . . . Tell you what, Henry. You go back over there and give Joe Benour the sign that we're gathering, and when I got the rest of 'em rousted out, we'll converge on the saloon."

Ben had been listening with increasing interest to this conversation and thought he knew what Slim and Bullerman were talking about. Town vigilantes. Most towns had them. Some never used them, some used them rarely, and sometimes they were mustered when the crisis did not really require them.

Bullerman continued to stand below the meager overhang gazing unhappily in the direction of the roadway. It was impossible to make anything out that far away. The rain was still coming down in sheets. It was moving from north to south; waves of water marching over a cowed countryside.

Henry Bullerman did not look happy when he said, "You really think we ought to, Slim?"

Slim straightened up off his hayfork. "He's in there alone, Henry, an' you said yourself Hearst is taking on a load of Dutch courage—with his whole damned crew."

Bullerman bobbed his head slowly, obviously reluctant. "Yeah. Well—I'll take the other side of town an' you take this side and—"

"Wait a minute," Ben said, interrupting the fat man. "Are you fellers talkin' about town vigilantes?"

Both Bullerman and Slim nodded.

Ben blew out a long breath before speaking again. "My guess is that Hearst is looking for me."

Bullerman said, "It don't take a lot of thinkin' to figure that out. . . . You and them Oakley boys, but mostly you."

"Then it's between him and me," Ben told them, and they both regarded him impassively as he told them the rest of it. "It's got to be settled. Personally, I wouldn't pick a night like this to settle it, but he's here and sooner or later he's going to come lookin' for me, so it's not my choice."

Slim spoke up. "I told you to go to bed early. We can handle this. There are ten townsmen. Eleven if Hoffman was here, but he ain't."

Ben regarded the tall, lean man. "Ten of you fellers and seven of them, countin' Hearst. You know what'll happen? A damned war."

"He rode in for trouble," stated Slim flatly. "We back the marshal. Every blessed one of us. An' we've had to do this before. . . . We use shotguns, cowboy. Maybe, like you say, it'll be a war, but I'll tell you one thing, it won't last long."

Ben stared at them. Bullerman did not look as though he relished any of this, but Slim Denham's jaw was set and his expression had a granite cast to it. "Slim, use your head," Ben said, above the sound of rain. "Marshal Calahan is in there too. You fellers go in there with shotguns and Calahan's goin' to be the first casualty."

Bullerman nodded his head, but said nothing. Slim squinted in Ben's direction, spat, then spoke. "You want to call Jess Hearst by yourself, with him in there with his six riders? You're crazy. It won't be Calahan that gets it, it'll be you."

Ben ignored that to address Bullerman. "Are their horses still tied up out front?" When Bullerman nodded, Ben shot a glance at the corralyard hostler. "It's rainin' like a fat cow peein' on a flat rock, Slim. You and me can take their horses down to the livery barn, yank the saddles and stall them. It's rainin' so hard Hearst won't hear us leading his animals away."

The liveryman turned his head slowly to stare at Ben Moore. "What the hell good is that goin' to do? Besides, when one of em' walks out he's goin' to holler that their horses are gone."

"We got to take that chance," stated Ben. "After we set those gents on foot, you two can go roust up your vigilantes while I'm gettin' inside the saloon from the back alley over behind the saloon. If it works, you townsmen with your scatterguns will have them from in front and I'll have them from in back."

Bullerman looked at Slim. "This is crazy," he said. It'll never work. It'll take too long and besides—"

"What can we lose?" asked Slim, and stepped away to lean his hayfork aside. "It's pretty farfetched, Henry, but if it works, the marshall will have himself a jailhouse full of cowboys. Let's you'n me go get those horses."

Bullerman opened his mouth to protest again but the stage company yardman nudged him roughly and started in the direction of the front gate, which was invisible until the three of them were within five feet of it. The rain should have been diminishing by now, but it wasn't. From the open gateway they could dimly discern orange lampglow down in front of the saloon. There did not seem to be any other lights along the full length of Main Street, but with visibility as limited as it was, there could have been ten more lighted windows and they would not have been discernible from the corralyard gateway.

The liveryman ignored Ben Moore and stared dispiritedly at Slim Denham. "Crazy," he muttered. The word was whipped away by the rain.

Slim grinned at Bullerman and Ben. "Let's go," he exclaimed and led off down into the chocolaty millrace that was the roadway.

Ben remained with them until all the tied horses were being led southward behind Bullerman and Slim, then he stepped into a dogtrot between two buildings where the full force of the storm could not reach him, and hoped as hard as he could that the men inside the saloon where it was comfortably warm and dry would not come out. They would have no incentive to unless Jess Hearst's rancor toward the stranger, who had bought in on the side of the Oakley children, became a whiskey-fed fury.

Ben wagged his head over Marshal Calahan being in there. Every graveyard west of the Missouri River had headstones to mark the resting places of lawmen with more courage than brains.

He went down the dogtrot into the back alley. The mud was deeper back there than it had been in the front roadway. There were runnels of water cutting channels. He was alert, otherwise he might not have seen the man moving from the inside of a three-sided shed in the direction of the saloon's back-alley door.

It was too late for Ben to duck back into the dogtrot. He reached for his handgun but did not draw it, hoping hard that the man plowing through the alleyway mud would not notice him if he stood perfectly still.

The dark silhouette moved swiftly once it was clear of the shed. The man was dry, so evidently he had not been out back for very long. His progress in the direction of the saloon doorway was neither steady nor straight, so Ben thought he knew why the man had come out here, and why he had gone into that shed.

The man was approaching the two low steps leading to the door when he paused to kick mud off his boots and to raise his head.

He saw Ben Moore, missed a strike against the steps with a muddy boot and called out, "Will, is that you?"

Ben drew the handgun, let it hang at his side and started toward the cowboy as he called back, "I never seen so much rain in my whole damned life." Ben was betting that the noise made by the rainfall would make his voice unrecognizable. It was a safe bet. This close to buildings, rain hammering over rooftops sounded like an entire regiment of drummers.

The man on the steps said, "What'n hell you doin' down there? Ain't no outhouse. Manure told us that."

Ben was close enough to raise the gun as he said, "You let Benour hear you call him that and . . . Now just don't move, mister. Not one damned step! Peel that gun out of its holster and drop it!"

The cowboy was too stunned to obey until Ben was within six feet of him and cocked his weapon. The cowboy dropped his gun into one of those runnels made by the rain. It was lost to sight almost instantly, its owner becoming sober very quickly as Ben gestured for him to walk back down into the alley.

The man obeyed. He was getting soaked. He had not bothered putting on his slicker when he left the saloon because he had not expected to be outside very long. He was shivering as Moore went up close and jerked his head sideways in the direction of the three-sided shed. The last thing he wanted was a prisoner, but he had one. As they were sloshing through muddy water to the shed, the prisoner said, "I got exactly six bits to my name, so you ain't goin' to fare very well robbin' me, friend."

The roof of the shed leaked, but even so it was drier inside than it was outside. The prisoner stopped and turned to face Ben. Even though it was dark inside the shed, the man said, "I'll be damned. I know you."

Ben could make out the other man's features too. "Yeah. The last time I tied you, your boss came along and turned you loose. I can't recollect your name."

"Pete Bruno."

Ben nodded. "Pete Bruno. Nice to see you again, Pete. What's that son of a bitch Hearst doing in there?"

Bruno relaxed slightly and hooked both thumbs in the front of his shellbelt as he replied. "He's pondering, I guess. We heard about them Oakley kids an' you when we rode in this evening. He owes you, mister. He made me swear not to tell the rest of the crew that you put out his lights in a fistfight. He's goin' to kill you on sight, and he's had enough whiskey tonight to do it."

Ben stood hipshot eyeing the cowboy. "Why do you ride for a man like that?" he asked.

Bruno shrugged. "Can you offer me more to ride for you? A job is a job, mister, an' while I'm ridin' for Mister Hearst I'm loyal to his brand, same as you'd be."

"Naw," growled Ben. "I'd quit before I'd ride for a man

who shoots at little kids an' steals what little their dead folks left them. . . . Turn around, Pete."

"Wait a minute, Mister Moore. Just tie me like you done before."

"Turn around!"

Pete began shuffling his feet but did not actually turn. "I've heard of fellers bein' killed by bein' hit over the head by someone who didn't know how hard to hit."

"Are you goin' to turn, or do I shoot you?"

Pete turned, then hunched up his shoulders, gritted his teeth and squeezed his eyes closed.

Ben dropped him like a pole-axed steer, then trussed Bruno as he had done before, by using the cowboy's own belts.

As Ben moved back out into the rain in the direction of the saloon's rear door, a hatted head appeared around the door and a man called out, "What'n hell took you so long, Pete? Jess is arguin' with the marshal. You better get your butt in here."

The speaker left the door ajar. Ben pushed it farther back and stepped into a storeroom of some kind with another door across the room. By the time he reached that one and got it opened, he did not realize that the thunderous rain roar on the roof was slackening off.

CHAPTER 13

Time to Sweat

BEN opened the storeroom door inch by inch until he could see the saloon-owner's back slightly to his left. Benour was behind the bar. Ben could see that Benour had one hand resting upon a shotgun. The gun was near the edge of a back-bar shelf.

No one was paying any attention to Benour. Across the room, barring the front exit, Marshal Calahan had taken a wide-legged stance. Directly in front of him was the much larger and heavier man who was recognizable even from the rear.

At the moment Ben had the door open far enough to see those three men, someone spoke from the left, where Ben could not see. "A man's got a right to look after hisself, Marshal, an' that feller named Moore—"

"Shut up, Morrison," Calahan said sharply. Then he spoke to Hearst. "I told you, Jess. You're not going to make trouble in town."

Hearst was hunched forward slightly. Ben did not have to see his face to know his mood. He eased the door open another few inches and could finally see three cowboys with their backs to the bar, slouching as they watched and waited.

Hearst raised an oaken arm. "For the last time," he said thickly to Marshal Calahan. "Get out of my way."

Calahan did not budge. "And you—all of you—will get on your horses and leave town."

Jess Hearst eased up to his full height. "Marshal, you're pushin' for it and you're goin' to get it!"

Ben could see the barman tighten his fingers around the sawed-off scattergun and lean back away from the bar as he was raising it. Every eye in the saloon was fixed upon the pair of antagonists over by the roadway door. No one heeded the unsmiling barman until he deliberately hauled back one shotgun hammer. Then hauled back the second one. If Ben had thought about it he would have understood how those sounds could have traveled as far as they did. The rainfall was lessening.

The cowboys turned their heads but remained facing their boss. Jess Hearst seemed to gather himself, to brace himself against what that sound implied.

Joe Benour leaned against the bar, shotgun in both hands. He turned it slightly in the direction of the motionless range riders. "Step clear of the bar and drop your weapons," he growled.

The Hearst riders obeyed. They would have been insane not to. At that range, a scattergun could have made mincemeat of them.

Jess Hearst turned very slowly. He was carrying a six-gun with an ivory handle. With one hand resting on the handle of the weapon, he glowered at Joe Benour. The barman was not easily intimidated. He shifted the gun slightly until it covered Hearst too. "You heard me, Jess. There won't be any trouble in here. Drop your handgun, then take your men and get the hell out of my saloon."

Hearst was red-faced. From Moore's hiding place he could see the cowman's features distinctly. Hearst had been drinking but he was a long way from being drunk. But right now he looked angry enough to take on Benour's shotgun.

Ben held his breath. There was not a man alive who could draw against a leveled shotgun with both hammers pulled back.

Calahan spoke into the silence as he moved very slowly to one side, which left the roadway doors accessible to Jess Hearst. "Drop the gun, Jess. He'll cut you in two with that thing."

Calahan could not see Hearst's eyes waver, jump to his

riders over by the bar, then back to Joe Benour, who was motionless, with one finger curled against a trigger inside the guard of his shotgun.

It was Hearst's decision. There was no longer any room for talk. Ben was hardly breathing right up to the moment when the big cowman raised his right arm very slowly while staring at the saloonman. He lifted away the Colt with its ivory handle and let it fall.

The sound as the heavy weapon struck the floor was loud. Ben's grip on the door latch loosened slightly as Marshal Calahan spoke. "You boys along the bar—mount up and head for home."

He had barely got that out when the roadway door was punched violently inward. Everyone's attention was caught and held by seven men carrying shotguns who pushed in out of the darkness. One of them, a man Ben did not recognize, shoved his double barrels against Hearst's back over the kidneys and none too gently forced the large man to move away from the door, toward the center of the room.

The last armed townsman to enter was Henry Bullerman. He squinted in the direction of the bar as though expecting to see Ben over there, then a vigilante cut across in front of Bullerman, distracting him as the vigilante went around the room picking up six-guns.

When he had them all he carried them to the bar, dumped them there and gestured in the direction of the roadway door with his scattergun. Ben had no difficulty recognizing Slim Denham from the corralyard.

"Line up," Slim snapped. As the Hearst riders were obeying, Slim looked at Marshal Calahan. "You want to lock them up?"

Calahan shook his head. "No. They can go, all but Jess. I'll take him down to the jailhouse with me." As Calahan finished speaking he jerked his head for the riders to leave the room. They did and moments later they were squawking like pigs caught in a gate. One man shoved his head back into the room and said, "Our horses are gone!"

Slim Denham answered caustically. "Anyone who'd leave horses tied like you fellers did, without any way for them to get some protection from the storm, don't deserve to even ride horses. Your animals are down at the livery barn. Get on them and get out of town."

Being alone among enemies took a lot of the starch out of Jess Hearst. Without looking at anyone he went to a chair and sank down.

Joe Benour gingerly let the hammers down on his shotgun and placed the weapon on its shelf, then stepped back to reach for an unopened bottle of malt whiskey, and set it in plain sight atop the bar as he said, "On the house, gents."

This time Henry Bullerman was the first man to reach the bar. Henry watched Marshal Calahan and Jess Hearst leave the saloon as the relieved and quite satisfied townsmen noisily bellied up to the bar.

Ben went back out into the dark alley and finally paused to raise his head. The rain had all but stopped, but now there was a bitterly cold wind blowing. He returned to the shed, freed the now conscious Pete Bruno, hoisted him to his feet and gave him a forward shove as he said, "It's all over. Hearst's riders are down at the livery barn saddling up. . . . Walk ahead of me until we come to the end of the alley, then go over an' join your friends. . . . One other thing, Pete. I meant it the other day when I said I'd shoot any Hearst rider I catch on the Oakley place. You remember that?"

Bruno had a throbbing headache. "I remember," he muttered. "And now you remember this: I don't know what happened, but I'll tell you for a damn fact the next time we meet, Mister Moore, it's going to be my turn."

Ben took that philosophically. When they reached an intersecting roadway he stopped to watch Pete Bruno walk in the direction of the livery barn.

He continued to stand there, a shadow among darker

shadows, until the Hearst riding crew went sloshing up out of Wileyville with that bitterly cold wind in their faces.

He crossed the road, stepped up onto the plankwalk and walked northward. In front of the lighted jailhouse he was tempted to stop, but Marshal Calahan probably would not appreciate having a third party in his office while he was reading the riot act to Jess Hearst, so Moore walked on past and got up as far as the open gates of the corralyard before noticing lighted windows up at Doctor Pittinger's place. He went there, knocked and was admitted by Elizabeth Hearst, whose face was flushed because the house was too warm.

He shed his poncho on the porch and left his sodden hat lying atop it before going into the parlor where lamplight made him squint.

Elizabeth eyed him before asking where he had been to get so wet and muddy. He countered her question with one of his own. "Where is the doctor?"

"On a call."

He stopped squinting. "This late at night?"

Her answer was short. "Inconvenience goes with his trade." She raised a small towel she'd been holding to her face to soak up some perspiration. "Do you want to see Arthur?"

"Isn't he sleeping?"

"Probably. He and Jamie played cards until a short while ago when I sent Jamie off to bed. But you can see him. I'm sure he'd like that."

Ben stood gazing at her. He had that same uncomfortable feeling he'd had the first time he'd seen her. A shiny face did not detract from her beauty.

"Maybe after a while," he told her and motioned toward a chair. When they were both seated he told her everything that had happened since the Hearst crew and their employer had ridden into Wileyville. She sat forward on her chair, clutching the small white towel as she listened.

When Ben was finished Elizabeth frowned faintly. "No

matter what my brother says to Jess Hearst, this won't be the end of it, Mister Moore."

He thought she might be right, but what he responded to now was her last two words. "When we were working together over Arthur, you were Elizabeth and I was Ben."

She lowered her eyes. He sat watching her and waiting. When it seemed she might not favor returning to a first-name basis, he spoke again. "That's all right, Elizabeth. If you want to start callin' me Mister Moore again, it's all right. That'll be your decision. Now, my decision is to go right on callin' you Elizabeth." He got to his feet. It was very warm in the house. "I think I ought to let Arthur sleep. I'll come around tomorrow."

She trailed him to the front door, and when he passed through and stopped on the porch to pick up his poncho and hat, she said, "All they want to talk about is you. How you can cook. How you treat them like their father did. How the three of you are going to buy cattle and be partners."

He smiled at her. "I've never been married. Never even came close to it. Likely I never will get married. But to be downright truthful with you, Elizabeth, I'm tired of riding north every spring to hire on and spend all summer workin' other folks' cattle. . . . This way, I'll have two sons—sort of, anyway. At least that's what I've been thinking."

"And think how nice it will be for you to have sons without having to put up with a wife," she said. "The boys will grow up without anyone telling them to wash behind their ears, not to chew tobacco, not to swear . . . a long list of things that make the difference between half-civilized rangemen and everyone else."

He smiled at her. "Yep. That's just about how they're goin' to grow up. Not having anyone tell them any of those things—except maybe about the chewin' tobacco. It made me sick as a dog the only time I ever tried it. I reckon I'll tell them about that."

He said goodnight and brushed his hat brim. Ben walked

down off the porch, through the little front gate and turned southward in the direction of the corralyard.

Slim Denham was sitting on the side of his bunk at the corralyard tugging off muddy boots and looked up when Ben walked in. Slim had a chair backed up to the popping stove with some soggy clothing draped over it to dry. Otherwise, the bunkhouse was hot enough to fry eggs on the floor.

As Slim dropped one boot and looked around for something to wipe his muddy hands on, he said, "It went off like clockwork, didn't it? Where was you?"

"Watching from the storeroom behind the bar. . . . It's awful damned hot in here, Slim."

Slim was grunting over the second boot and did not reply until he had the boot off, then he sat wiggling his toes as he said, "The left boot leaks like a sieve. Did you talk to the marshal after he herded young Hearst to the jailhouse?"

Ben gave up about the heat, went to his bunk and began peeling off damp clothes. "No. I went up to see how the boys are getting along."

"How's the youngest one—what's his name?"

"Arthur. I didn't want to waken them but Elizabeth said they were doing fine."

Slim found someone's abandoned undershirt in a corner and used it to wipe his hands with. "Elizabeth? You mean Calahan's sister, the café-lady?"

"Yeah. She's the only Elizabeth I know in Wileyville."

Slim returned to his bunk and sat down. "There's a few more around. Do you call her Elizabeth to her face?"

"Yes. Is there a reason why I shouldn't?"

"Well, *I* don't an' I've never heard anyone else do it except her brother."

Ben dragged an old bench close to the stove and put his clothing to dry also. Then he gazed at the corralyard hostler. After all they had been through tonight, Slim elected to settle on the least important thing to discuss. Ben went back to his bunk.

He was poised to roll up onto his back and sleep when Slim spoke again. "I got to tell you that although I sided with your plan against Bullerman, I really didn't think it'd work."

Ben opened his eyes and stared at the log wall. "It wasn't a good plan but darned if I could think of anything else—unless it was for me to march into the saloon and call Hearst."

Slim got settled under his blankets and sighed loudly as he composed himself for sleep. "If you'd done that, partner, let me tell you something: Hearst an' his crew would have chewed you up and spit you out."

"Maybe. Good night, Slim."

"Good night, Ben. . . . Elizabeth—to her face?"

CHAPTER 14

The Day After

JOB Upton heard about the showdown at the café, where no one mentioned anything else. By the time he got up to the corralyard he was smiling, and when he went back where Slim and Ben were drying the backs of some harness horses with croaker sacks before harnessing them, Job was in an excellent mood. He did not waste any time asking for details. Slim told him while Ben continued to work over the horses, but when Slim had told his version, Upton turned on Ben. "Where was you?"

"In the storeroom behind the bar watching through a half-open door."

Upton gazed from one of them to the other, then wagged his head. "Damnedest thing I've heard about in years. What'd the marshal say to young Hearst?"

They did not know so Job Upton struck out for his office to do a little paper work before he hunted up the lawman.

The same thing happened when Doctor Pittinger got back to town about daybreak and left his rig and animal to be cared for at the livery barn. He saw Ben and Slim finishing up the hooking of a four-horse hitch to a stagecoach and walked into the yard for the particulars. All he knew was what the livery barn nightman had told him, and that was just enough to get Pittinger fired up.

Ben and Slim repeated their stories, Pittinger listened with an expression of increasing approval, and before leaving he said he would stand the drinks the next time they met over at Benour's saloon.

Just once, immediately after they saw the whip take his coach and four out into the roadway for a southward run,

105

did Denham mention last night's confrontation. That was when he told Ben that unless Marshal Calahan locked up Jess Hearst and buried the key, what happened last night was going to be the opening round with more to come.

Ben had already thought about this. "It's up to him. He knows by now that I said I'd shoot any Hearst rider I found on the Oakley place."

Slim's eyes widened. "What in hell did you say that for? That's an invitation. You don't know young Hearst. He thrives on things like that."

Ben shrugged and watched Marshal Calahan come out of the saloon and turn southward in the direction of the general store. He didn't see whether Calahan entered or not. Someone sang out Ben's name from across the road in front of the gunsmith's shop. It was Pete Bruno, and the fact that he had not left town last night with the other Hearst riders interested Ben, who told Slim who the man was over in front of the gun shop. Slim was also surprised. Bruno was heading through the mud to their side of the roadway.

Bruno halted a couple of yards away, lifted his hat and lowered his head. He had a very professional-looking bandage where someone had shaved away the hair.

Ben was not wholly sympathetic but he resisted saying that he had held back a little when he hit the cowboy over the head.

Jeff Hoffman, the stage driver, came down into town from the north. He was sitting slouched and moving just his jaws as he aimed for the gateway. He entered the yard with Slim on his left side, Ben and the Hearst rider on the far side. Slim walked toward the middle of the yard to care for the rig and animals, leaving Ben down at the gate with Pete Bruno.

Slim had a hunch that Pete Bruno had not ridden out with the Hearst men last night because he had quit. He was correct; that was what Bruno was telling Ben as they stood to one side of the log gateway with a faint lacing of heat coming into the cloudless day.

When Bruno explained that he had quit Hearst last night down at the livery barn, he leaned against a log gate and used a twig to prise mud from between his undershot boot heel and the boot sole. Ben eyed him thoughtfully. The one thing Bruno had not mentioned was why he had halloaed to Ben from across the road.

After Bruno finished talking, Ben said, "Then you'll be riding out, and that's one less I'll have to keep an eye peeled for."

Bruno straightened up and tossed the twig aside. "Well, maybe. That depends." He showed a raffish smile. "We heard around town last evenin' that you figured to stock the Oakley place."

Ben nodded. "That's the plan. I don't know how the banker'll feel about the idea, though."

Bruno ignored the remark about the banker. "How many head you expect that place will run?"

"More than I'll be able to buy. But maybe over the years we can hold back heifers and build it up. Why—you know where there are some cattle for sale?"

"Nope. What I was figuring was that even with them two kids you can't handle four, five hunnert head by yourself."

Understanding finally arrived for Ben. He glanced into the yard where Slim and Jeff Hoffman were arguing about something, then he looked back at the rangeman. "Maybe next year, and most likely sure as hell the year after, but right now I couldn't pay wages. I got exactly four dollars to my name." Ben paused as a thought struck him. He narrowed his eyes slightly. "Pete, the next outfit you hire out to had ought to be at least a hundred miles from here. If I could hire you on, and Hearst saw you riding for the Arrowhead Cattle Company, he'd waylay you and overhaul your rigging until you couldn't stand up."

Bruno smiled. "You got him figured right. But Jess has given me the dirty end of the stick for about a year now. Besides that, I don't like some of the things he's done."

Ben put a shrewd stare upon the cowboy. "Like shootin' at children?"

"Yeah. That and some other underhanded things."

"Pete, I was told you was along and shot at them too."

Bruno snapped erect. "Not on your life. If I'd been with Jess that day he'd have had to whup me senseless to keep me from keepin' him from doing that."

"Do you know who the second man was?"

"Sure, I know. It was Bob Morrison."

"Do you two look alike?"

"Same size and heft, I expect. Maybe from a distance someone might mistake him for me. . . . No sir, I never shot at no children in my life."

Ben smiled at the rider, while behind that smile he was making judgments about Pete Bruno. Not about whether to hire him, because that was impossible, but about whether Bruno had really quit—and whether he had been left behind to strike up a conversation with Ben and learn his plans. Ben did not believe for one minute Jess Hearst was above doing that. What he was trying to make a decision about was whether Pete Bruno was like that too.

He repeated what he had said earlier about being unable to pay a hired hand and would have walked back into the yard to help Slim with the freight wagon and its mule-hitch, but Bruno stopped him. He was not smiling or being affable now. "About the time I hired on last year them folks over at the Oakley place died. I heard bits an' pieces about them. Didn't pay much attention. It wasn't none of my affair. I come back in from lookin' to make sure the bulls was stayin' with the cows an' Jess called me out back where him and Bob Morrison had about forty cattle in the working corrals. They'd already put the Hearst mark on about half of them."

Ben interrupted. "What is the Hearst brand?"

"Crossed arrows. . . . I went back there and helped. The stock they was workin' already had one mark. Looked like a tree."

Ben faintly smiled and nodded. "The Oakley brand?"

"I don't know—It could have been. . . . When we'd run them tree-branded cattle in to be marked with Hearst's mark, Jess or Bob, whichever was closest to the fire, would yank out a bar-brand and run it diagonal across the tree brand."

"Then they'd put on Hearst's brand?"

"Yep. I didn't ask where Jess had got them oak-tree cattle and neither he nor Bob told me. I'd never seen that brand before an' didn't think much about it until I was in town last summer and got to talkin' to the blacksmith. He told me he'd made just about every branding iron in the country. I asked him if he'd ever made a tree brand. He said he'd made two of 'em, a big one for cattle an' a smaller one for horses. He said he'd made them for Oakley."

Ben ran a slow glance back up into the yard where Slim and Jeff Hoffman were pushing the freight wagon to the south side of the yard where other vehicles were parked. Slim had already cared for the mules. He returned his attention to Pete Bruno. He was satisfied about one thing: Bruno never in God's green world would have told Ben about those stolen cattle if he was still working for Jess Hearst. "How about horses?" he asked.

"I can't say. The Hearst ranch runs a hell of a lot of horses. Upwards of maybe a hunnert and fifty head. Was they branded too?"

Ben did not think so. "I doubt it."

Bruno turned aside to expectorate before saying, "He was a damned fool not to, with a neighbor like Jess Hearst." Pete narrowed his eyes and studied Ben for a moment before he spoke again. "Tell you what, Mister Moore, I'll hire on for the winter feedin' and all, an' you can pay me when you get that loan from old Custis the banker. I like this country. But maybe come next spring I'll get the itch to head north again. In the meanwhile if you'll feed me and your bunkhouse roof don't leak, I'd just as soon get paid later as set around Wileyville until my money runs out."

Ben thought it over. For a fact he would need another man when he got the cattle. He repeated what he had said earlier. "Jess Hearst'll hang your hide out to dry if he sees you riding for us."

Bruno did not deny that, he just stood there smiling, with his thumbs hooked in his shellbelt. "I'll keep my eyes open. I'll tell you one thing, if he's armed and comes alone, he won't have a prayer of a chance. I've seen him draw. If he don't come alone, why then, like you say, he'll most likely hang my hide out to dry. If you need a hired hand, I'm willin' to take a chance on the rest of it."

Ben shoved out a callused, thick hand. Pete Bruno met it halfway. Ben explained why he was hanging around town. Pete already knew why. He said, "How long before the lad can stand the ride back to the ranch?"

"Maybe the end of this week, maybe the end of next week. But I suppose you'n I could ride out there after I see the banker, and get things ready."

Bruno was agreeable to that. "Let me know when you want to ride an' I'll hire an animal from the fat liveryman. Jess took the Hearst horse I rode into town on."

The morning coach arrived, cut a wide swath so as to miss either gate with wheel hubs and pulled to a dead stop out where morning sunshine was finally beginning to have heat.

Pete Bruno crossed the road in the direction of the pool hall. Ben watched him go, wondered why he had agreed to hire Bruno, then turned as the whip climbed to the ground and bellowed for a yardman.

There were three passengers. Two women traveling together and one man, probably a preacher because he had his celluloid collar on backward.

Slim arrived after the passengers were out of the yard. Ben already had the horses free of their singletrees and doubletrees. As he and Slim led the horses toward shade near the harness room, Ben caught a whiff of Slim's breath. To Ben it seemed almost indecent for folks to drink before their midday meal, but that was probably because Ben was not much of a drinker and never had been. As for Slim Denham, Ben had never seen him even unsteady so Ben assumed Slim didn't take more than a nip or two during the day.

They had the horses cared for and turned into a round corral to roll, tank up at the trough and start lipping around for stray hay stalks, when Marshal Calahan came into the yard, nodded and said, "Did you round up the vigilantes last night, Slim?"

Slim nodded.

The marshal looked steadily at him for a moment, then spoke again. "You know the rules. Before they're called out you're supposed to get my agreement."

With a little wry smile on his face, Slim replied, "Seems to me you was too busy watchin' those fellers to be interrupted. . . . It worked, didn't it?"

Calahan's black eyes faintly twinkled. "Yeah, it sure worked." He turned toward Ben Moore. "Joe Benour was a little upset this morning when someone said they saw you standin' in his storeroom doorway, behind him, with a cocked gun in your hand."

Ben was surprised that he had been seen. "That was the idea—me behind them, the town vigilantes in front of them."

Marshal Calahan grinned ruefully, reset his hat and was turning to depart when he said, "Elizabeth would like to see you sometime today, whenever you can shake loose for a few minutes."

Ben nodded and turned to go check the troughs. Slim was standing there like he'd taken root. "You wasn't makin' that up last night, about callin' her Elizabeth. I'll be double-damned."

Ben smiled and walked away. He spent the rest of the morning cleaning green scum from stone troughs, pitching feed and strolling among the horses looking for shoes that needed replacing.

The sky was flawless and for an autumn day with winter

close, it was unseasonably hot. Ben went out back, stripped down and bathed in a leaky old wooden trough, emptied the thing and returned to the front of the yard looking for Slim to see which one of them went to supper first.

Job Upton came through the rear doorway of his office. He met Ben Moore halfway and, because it was his custom to be straightforward and blunt, he offered none of the customary opening remarks that were standard in cattle country. He simply said, "Jeff Hoffman quit. He's been talkin' about doin' it so long I never thought he would. But he quit this morning." Upton paused. "I don't have another driver to deliver some freight southwest of town to the Brittany ranch. . . . You're gettin' hostler wages, which is about half what whips gets, but if you'll take the freight out there I'll pay you whip's wages."

Ben frowned. "When?"

"Well, they want that stuff out there today. But I can lie a little so's you can start out about dawn tomorrow."

"How far is this Brittany ranch?"

Job Upton gestured. "You go south of town, go down to the first mileage marker, an' directly across from it are some ruts. That's the Brittany road. The headquarter buildings are about four miles southwest. You can't get lost if you stay in the ruts." Job raised dark eyebrows. "For driver's pay? I got no one else to send an' I'd take it kindly if you'd do it."

"All right. I got to have dinner first."

Job looked relieved. "Sure. You go ahead an' eat an' I'll hunt up Slim to help me get the outfit ready. . . . I'm obliged to you."

On the way to the café Ben smiled to himself; Job had acted like a man to whom pleading came hard.

Ben entered the café as two rangemen were departing. They nodded and turned up in the direction of the saloon. Up there, one of them turned to gaze back down in the direction of the café.

Ben had the counter to himself except for an old man

drinking soup from a large bowl at the extreme lower end of the counter.

Elizabeth's face was shiny when she stood in front of him with the counter between them. He smiled at her. "Whatever you got that I can put down an' that will stay down."

It was a tired joke, one that she had heard an interminable number of times. Without smiling back she said, "Antelope steak, fresh bread, blueberry pie, and coffee?"

His eyes widened slightly. "Blueberry pie?"

"The Indians who live in shacks in back of town go into the mountains and pick them. No one else knows where they go. All right?"

He nodded. "I guess so. It'll have to stick to my ribs. I'm goin' to haul freight out to the Brittany ranch."

She looked steadily at him for a moment, then went back to her kitchen. He watched the toothless old man for a while, then leaned both arms atop the counter and went musingly back through what had happened last night in Joe Benour's place.

He was still thinking about that when Elizabeth brought his meal. When he looked up at her she avoided his gaze and returned briskly to the cooking area. She seemed slightly breathless.

He was puzzled by her mood, but went to work on his meal without trying to guess what had caused the change in her.

The old gaffer arose, put a nickel beside his empty bowl and shuffled toward the door. When he was behind Moore he squinted hard, then turned back with a question. "You the young feller who saved the lad's life nightafore last?"

Ben smiled. "I was one of them."

"You done good, son. You done exactly right. I thought old Fred done taken them with him."

Ben twisted around. "Did you know old Fred?"

The old man chuckled, displaying toothless gums. "Know Fred? Yas, a man might say I knowed him. We played black-jack ever' Sattidy night for some years." The old man raised a grimy cuff to wipe his lips. "I know what they're sayin'. That Fred run off an' abandoned them little boys. . . . There's got to be more to it than that. I knowed Fred well enough to doubt he'd do somethin' like that. . . . Well, nice talkin' to you."

The old man shuffled out of the café, and Ben turned back to his meal.

CHAPTER 15

A Nice Day for Hauling Freight

ELIZABETH'S blueberry pie was something a man would write home about. Ben was normally a fast eater, but he sat enjoying that pie right up to the moment Marshal Calahan walked in, sat down, shoved his hat back and watched Ben scoff up the last crumbs. Calahan said, "Good, was it?"

Ben wagged his head. "Best I ever ate."

Elizabeth came down the counter to take her brother's order. Ben was fishing in a trouser pocket for silver and did not see the long look that passed between the Calahans. As Elizabeth stopped in front of Ben on her way to the kitchen, she smiled. "I'm glad you liked the pie," she said.

"Your cookin' would be enough to make a man never want to leave Wileyville."

She reddened and walked away. Ben followed her with his eyes for a moment, then turned a bewildered look to her brother. Marshal Calahan simply shrugged his shoulders and went on eating. "Women," he said around a mouthful of food. "It's like figuring the weather. When you're sure you know what they'll do, they do just the opposite." Calahan swallowed and reached for his coffee cup. "Heard you were takin' freight out to the Brittany ranch."

Ben nodded his head, suspecting Calahan had got his information from the corralyard. He was wrong.

"Be a nice drive on a day like this."

"What is it, about six, seven miles?"

"Yes, I'd guess that'll be about right. What are you hauling?"

115

"Furniture. At least that's what Job Upton told me. Maybe if I'm lucky I'll be able to get back to town about supper time."

Ben arose, put coins beside his platter and was turning to depart when Elizabeth appeared. Her face was not as shiny now and her luxurious mass of hair had been swept severely back and brushed until it shone. She had high color and when she addressed Ben Moore she looked at something on the wall over his right shoulder. "The boys missed you. I visited them this morning before opening the café. Could you spend a little time with them today?"

He watched her brother lean to look into his cup as he replied. "Like I said, Elizabeth, I got to haul freight out to the Brittany place. I'm sorry. . . . If it's not too late when I get back tonight I could go up there. How are they?"

"Jamie is restless. He needs open country. He'll never be a town person."

"Arthur?"

Her eyes drifted back and met his. "Arthur is getting better, but the child has been through a lot—and I don't mean his sickness. Bad enough to lose his mother, but he's also lost his father and grandfather. Arthur is the kind of child who needs someone."

Ben felt heat in his cheeks and glanced at Marshal Calahan, who was cleaning up his platter with a piece of bread and seemed totally disinterested in their discussion. But Ben Moore had not come down in the last rain. The marshal had not missed a word.

He turned his attention back to the handsome woman. "The boys and I will be partners in the Arrowhead Cattle Company."

"They need a father, Ben. You could adopt them."

Later, he could not decide which had shocked him the most—what she had said or that she had called him by his first name. Right now, though, she was waiting for an answer. He did not look at her when he gave it.

"We'll see, Elizabeth. We'll see. Now I better get over yonder."

After Ben Moore's departure, Tom Calahan arose and gazed in the direction of the door as he said to his sister, "He looked like you'd just flung a bucket of ice water in his face." Calahan smiled and counted out the coins for his meal. He was still smiling when he turned toward the door. His sister stopped him with a question. "Are you going to take someone with you?"

"Nope. You think I should?"

"Yes."

Calahan nodded. "I'll think on it. By the way, Moore was right. That was the best blueberry pie I ever tasted. You know what happens when you do something like that? Everyone expects you to do the exact same thing every time you make a pie."

As the law officer was pushing past the door his sister said, "Tom, you be careful."

If Marshal Calahan heard that, he gave no indication of it. His attention was fixed on a freight wagon behind a large pair of draft horses. The wagon was old, and although its sideboards had once been green, they were now the indeterminate shade of faded creek-bed rock. The horses had to weigh at least eighteen hundred pounds each, which meant that the load Moore was taking out of town was heavy.

Ben saw the lawman watching. When they came abreast each of them waved, then the café door opened and Elizabeth stepped up beside her tall brother to also watch the wagon pass closer to the southern end of town. She said nothing. Neither did her brother until he was ready to cross Main Street, then he roughly patted her shoulder as he said, "Don't fret, Liz."

She looked at him. "I can't help it, Tom. You know that. I'm a worrier."

He smiled. "Sure. Well, this time you got no call. I'll be down there before he even gets close."

"Maybe it'll be a wild goose chase."

He said, "Maybe," and kept on walking.

The sun was high and hot. It was sucking moisture out of the earth at a rapid pace. The roadway was still soft enough for wagon tracks to cut down into it, especially a laden wagon, but unless it rained again soon, the roadway would be dry in another day or two.

Ben did not worry; the draft horses whose big rumps he was watching could have pulled twice as much of a load as they were pulling. They did not even sweat until he had the mileage marker in sight, and then it was a fair guess that they broke a sweat more from the sun than from straining.

He had thought of taking Pete Bruno along. What made him consider that was Bruno himself. He had been leaning on an upright post in front of the gunsmith's shop when Ben left the corralyard. They had exchanged a wave, and that was when he thought of taking Pete along. But he hadn't.

Opposite the stone mileage marker were the ruts Job Upton had mentioned. He left the stage road, felt the wheels settle into the ruts and told the big horses that if they wanted to pick up the gait a little it would be fine with him. But they didn't, and Ben did not make them. He leaned to loop the lines around the binder handle and sat back. He had never been over the countryside below Wileyville, but it looked pretty much like the land he had come to know. It had rolling land swells, plenty of feed, and an occasional deep arroyo with thickets growing down where there was shade most of the day, and perhaps water not very far below the surface because all the scrub brush and trees down in those places seemed to be thriving.

He settled back on the seat and tipped down his hat. The horses would follow the ruts. Unless, of course, something spooked them—a bobcat, a cougar, or maybe a bear. But he was not concerned. Bears did not get this far from timber, berry bushes, and grub-filled deadfalls. Cougars also preferred an area where they could fade from human sight.

Bobcats might be out here. They ate a lot of mice, and this kind of grassland had plenty of them.

But bobcats would run from even the sight of the big horses and the wagon. And man smell.

He was between wakefulness and sleep when the horses pointed ahead and slightly southward with their ears. Ben sat up, shoved back his hat and followed their line of sighting. He saw nothing. Not even a coyote.

He settled back again, slouched along another mile or so, and this time when the horses lifted their heads, Ben saw a distant rider covering ground at an easy lope. He was heading southwesterly. Probably one of the Brittany rangemen. Ben scanned the area where the horseman had come from and decided the man had been down in one of those deep arroyos, which would account for the horses not seeing him sooner.

He did not speculate on why the rider had been down there, he got comfortable again and tipped down his hat to protect his eyes, and this time he would have dozed, except for the thought that kept him from it.

Had adoption been Elizabeth's idea, or the Oakley boys'? Adopting them wasn't necessary anyway; they were partners. The three of them.

He shoved these musings aside and concentrated on another subject. He had seen the Wileyville banker, knew his name was Bart Custis and had decided that his reserved expression was like that of most bankers Ben had encountered. If a man did not need money, they would lend him some. If a man did need it, they'd want a hell of a lot of collateral.

Ben sat straight up. He could use the Oakley place as collateral! That sudden thought came so quickly and solidly he did not notice that the horses were bending around southward, still in the ruts. By the time he realized this he was only indifferently interested. He could probably borrow enough on the ranch to get a good start and leave some in a bank account to boot.

The heat-induced drowsiness left him. He was wide-awake and alert when he could distantly make out a group of buildings in a setting of cottonwood trees that appeared to have been planted as a windbreak. In this kind of open country, if the wind blew at all, it blew like a son of a bitch. Whoever Mister Brittany was, he had planted those big trees a long time ago. They cast shade over most of the yard and in particular they shaded what Ben assumed was the main house, the Brittany residence.

He had plenty of time to stand up and study the buildings. There was no one in the yard, but there did not have to be if this was a working cow outfit. The crew would not appear until close to supper time.

He could not see the corrals behind the barn without leaving the ruts, which he did not do, so he had no idea whether that rider he had seen had turned his horse into one of the corrals or not.

The closer Ben got, the more desolate and empty the buildings seemed to be. There was a brooding silence down there. By now someone should have seen him coming, even if they hadn't been expecting a freight wagon from town.

No one appeared in the yard or upon the porch of the main house, the smaller porch of the log bunkhouse, or the larger, encircling porch of the cookhouse.

There should have been at least one dog barking by now. Ben unlooped the lines, evened them up and held them in gloved hands as he remained standing up.

He found parallels between his ranch, which had also been deserted and this place, which supposedly was not deserted. Right up to the time he entered the yard, angling toward the tie rack in front of the barn, halted the team and climbed down to unsnap the check reins and use them to loop around the tie post, he neither heard anything nor saw anyone.

There had to be someone here. Otherwise why would Job Upton have sent Ben down here with crates of furniture?

He finished securing the big horses but remained on the off-side of the rack looking around. The plausible explanation seemed to be that someone had just bought this place and had gone off to buy cattle to stock it with.

He straightened up off the pole feeling relieved. That was it; the furniture was for that big old log main house at the opposite end of the yard.

He stepped around from where the big horses had hidden him, and someone yelled, "*You!*"

Two seconds later there was a gunshot. Ben crouched when the second gunshot erupted. Both shots had come from carbines. Their sound was different from either a six-gun or a rifle. It was higher, more waspish.

Ben ducked for the barn opening. It was about forty feet away. He made a final lunge and got inside the barn at about the same moment another carbine shot blew the silence apart, and this time Ben heard the solid impact of lead against logwood.

He moved to the south side of the gloomy old barn and craned around until he could see where the bullet had torn loose a long splinter from the barn log, exposing raw wood beneath.

That time, one of those people with Winchesters had sure as hell been firing at him!

The big horses had set back a little at that third gunshot, but when there was no more shooting they came up on their tethers, eyes wide, nostils distended for soft snorting.

Ben was unaware of the beading sweat until it rolled down his nose and he had to fling it off. It was really not that hot this time of year, even when a man stood out in direct sunlight.

The silence returned, bringing with it that same brooding hush that had made Ben uneasy a short while before.

CHAPTER 16

The Brittany Yard

IT was one thing to be under personal attack by someone a man could see, and something quite different to be fired at by someone he could not see and probably would be unable to recognize if he could see him.

But there was a lead-pipe cinch: whoever the man was who had tried to hit him as he raced for shelter inside the barn had been trying to kill him, and folks didn't do that unless they had a reason to try it.

He rubbed his jaw in bafflement. There were two of them, but the one who had called out and who evidently had also fired a saddlegun did not appear to have been shooting in the direction of Ben and the barn.

He looked around, noted the wide and doorless rear barn opening and stopped speculating in order to find better protection than he had.

There were four horse stalls along the north side of the barn. Between the uppermost stall and the front opening there was a low, cribbed manger with tie-rope holes bored at intervals along the front of it. That was where someone had tied horses.

On the opposite side of the barn there was a box-like small enclosed room that probably had been for saddlery and harness, as well as a barrel or two of rolled barley. Most barns had those little enclosed places. Ben considered getting inside. There would be an advantage. Aside from being protected by four walls, when he did nothing, whoever had fired at him would have to hunt for him, and the moment he entered the barn, Ben, with only a six-gun, would get his chance.

The room's thick oak door had a massively forged latch with a very large brass lock hooked through it. Ben blew out a breath; so much for the idea of hiding in there.

He probably could have shot the lock off, and if he had the bushwhacker out there somewhere would probably have started stalking him, if he was not already doing it.

He considered the loft ladder, which was simply a log set into the ground, bolted at the top, with steps made of rough scantlings nailed up it at regular intervals. If he went up there, and the bushwhacker entered the barn and did not see Ben, he would not have to speculate for long to know where Ben was, and the only way out of the mow was by that same ladder.

He entered the horse stall nearest the rear barn opening, faded back in cool gloom and waited. He probably would not hear the gunman approaching because of moist earth, but he would see him if he came up to the doorway.

It was a very long wait. During it Ben sweated, grew restless and leaned in the shadows making some guesses about who the gunman was, and when he had to abandon that line of thinking, he settled on a suspicion that somehow, some way, this was one of Jess Hearst's tricks. Traps, more accurately.

But that did not explain the shot the bushwhacker had traded with someone else.

Ben gave it up, moved to the warped wooden front of his stall and peeked between two boards. He could see some corrals out there behind the barn and slightly southward, and he had an excellent view of the doorway.

There was no movement, no sign of anyone, not even a horse, if there was one in those corrals. He mopped off sweat, dried his gun hand down the outer seam of his britches and regripped the weapon. Suppose the bushwhacker had decided that since he had been unable to kill Ben with his first shot, he would ride away to await another better opportunity?

Ben stiffened. How had that son of a bitch known Ben

would be out here? The marshal had known he was going to come out, so did Job Upton and presumably so did Slim Denham—and Elizabeth. Not Elizabeth, she wouldn't have told whoever was probably stalking him right this minute.

Not knowingly anyway, but that didn't alter the fact that there was a killer out yonder, over in the area of the main house. At least he had been when the firing had started. They were both over there—whoever in hell they were.

Very suddenly a man's gravelly voice called out, "You move so much as one eye and I'll blow your head off!"

Ben heard each word very distinctly. The sound had come from out back and slightly southward, perhaps in the area of those pole corrals. There was no reply. In fact there was not another sound for what seemed like an hour, then what sounded pretty much like the same voice called out again. "Hey, Ben—you all right in there?"

Moore smiled bleakly to himself. If he answered, the caller would know exactly where he was. He did not reply.

A little later the gravelly voice shouted again. "Ben! This is Tom Calahan. Did he hit you when you ran for the barn?"

Moore sagged. The voice certainly sounded like that of the Wileyville town marshal. "No," he called back, "he didn't hit me."

"Come on out the back of the barn. He's tied like a turkey."

Ben eyed the ajar stall door but made no move toward it. "Trouble is," he called back, "I don't know what the hell this is all about, and I'm not goin' to walk right into someone's gun muzzle."

Calahan's voice was less strident this time. "Yeah. I don't blame you. . . . Liz cut out the alley doorway of the café and ran over to my office while you were eating. She told me where you were going, then she scampered back an' I walked over to hear it from you. All right?"

Ben felt like swearing. He had been thinking some very uncharitable thoughts about Job Upton and Slim Denham. "You just walk to the middle of the rear doorway where I can see you," Ben yelled, and eased up to the wide crack between warped old boards where he had looked out earlier.

Marshal Calahan came into sight, walking slowly and holding an uncocked six-gun at his side. He stopped, faced ahead and waited.

Ben said, "Drop the gun, Marshal."

Calahan's dark brows lowered blackly. "What's the matter with you? I had nothin' to do with this ambush."

"Is that a fact? How did it happen you were out here ahead of me? When I left town you were standing in front of the café."

"I saddled up right after you cleared town, rode hard west, then used the arroyos to get down here southward. . . . And this other feller didn't see me because I came in from the west behind the barn an' he was waiting at the northeast front corner of the main house. . . . Ben, we're wasting time."

Ben holstered his weapon and walked out of the stall, unaware that his shirt front clung to him, soggy with sweat. Marshal Calahan jerked his head. "Come along. I'll show you."

The man lying on his stomach in the trampled grass in front of a large corral gate made no effort to look up as they approached, so Calahan leaned and roughly rolled him onto his back. There were two guns in the grass, a Colt and a Winchester.

Ben knew the man. Not by name but by sight. He was powerfully put together, wore an unkempt dragoon moustache that was very light colored, and his pale blue eyes fixed themselves on Ben Moore.

Calahan jutted his jaw. "His name's Morrison. He rides for Jess Hearst." Calahan went closer and squatted. "Tell you what," he said to the man bound with rope. "You got one of two choices. Either you tell us what this is all about, or you'll take it to hell with you." Calahan drew his six-gun, shoved it to within six inches of the bushwhacker's face and cocked it.

Morrison's Adam's apple bobbed up and down twice, his

normally ruddy complexion paled. He raised his eyes from the gun to Calahan's face. "You wouldn't do it. It'd be murder an' you're a lawman."

Ben was staring at the gun too. When Calahan answered Morrison, Ben's gaze went to his face. Calahan was faintly smiling. "I'll do it. Don't you think for one minute that I won't. You shot at me around behind the main house. Your gun's got an empty casing in it." Ben held his breath as he watched the lawman's finger curl closer around the trigger.

Morrison's eyes returned to the weapon. At that distance a .45 slug would make mush out of a man's head. "All right," he said in a husky tone. "Let me go set against the back of the barn."

Calahan yanked loose the ankle rope and pushed his prisoner roughly toward the barn. He taunted him. "Run, Morrison. Make a break for it."

The bushwhacker ignored Calahan, turned around and sank down against the shaded rear log wall of the barn. He looked up at Ben. "You thirsty? I sure am."

Ben had forgotten about his thirst. Calahan sank to one knee, eased down the hammer of his Colt and leathered it. "Talk," he said to his prisoner. "Right from the start. How did you know Moore would be out here today? That'll do for openers."

Morrison dripped sweat that he could not brush off with both arms tied behind his back. "I didn't know he'd be out here, but Jess did."

Ben also sank to one knee. Calahan relaxed a little, obviously pleased with Morrison's statement. "How did Jess know he'd be out here?"

"I'd sure admire to have a drink of water, Marshal."

Calahan was unrelenting. Being shot at was not something he could forgive quickly. "How did Jess know Ben would be out here?"

"I'm tellin' you the gospel truth, Marshal; I got no idea how he knew. All I know is that he told me someone'd be out here with a freight wagon sometime today, and so help me, I been squattin' behind that damned house since I got down here this morning. I was about to give up when I saw the wagon and those big horses. . . . But by gawd I didn't see you comin'. Not until I looked back along the rear of the house an' there you was, tippy-toein' toward me with a Winchester in your hand."

Ben stood up, eyeing the old stone trough with water trickling into it from a dented lead pipe. There was green scum around the edges of the trough, but where the water came out of the pipe it looked clean.

Calahan also arose. He saw Ben eyeing the trough and said, "There's a canteen on my saddle over inside the shoeing shed." He waited until Ben was going back up through the barn toward the old outbuildings on the far side of the yard, then he looked dispassionately at his prisoner and wagged his head. "Now'd be a good time for you to make a run for it, Morrison."

The bushwhacker's pale eyes were fixed on Calahan when he replied. "Not on your damned life. You want to shoot me, it's goin' to be with my hands tied in back an' me sittin' on the ground—Moore's no fool. He'll know what happened."

Calahan changed the subject. "Jess wants the Oakley place pretty bad."

Morrison nodded his head.

"Why the hell didn't he just up and offer to buy it from Moore?"

This time Morrison put his head slightly to one side and looked wryly at the lawman. "You know him as well as I do. We been runnin' stock on the Oakley place since it was abandoned. After a man's done that for a while he sort of thinks he owns it. And Jess ain't like his paw; he wouldn't give the time of day for the Oakley place because he figures he don't have to. Accordin' to his lights, it's already his."

"So he sent you to bushwhack Moore," stated Calahan, and

raised his head to listen as Ben Moore led the big harness horses into the barn and stabled them with the harness on.

Morrison said nothing about being sent down here to kill Moore. When Ben walked out back with the lawman's canteen and handed it to Calahan, the lawman stepped close, trickled the cold water over his prisoner's shirtfront, then stepped back, smiling.

"How much did he pay you to kill Moore?"

Morrison's eyes were on the canteen when he replied. "I told you. I didn't know it'd be Moore. Just whoever was drivin' the wagon."

Ben spoke to the lawman. "Let him have some water."

Calahan stepped over and leaned. Morrison swallowed as water was trickled into his mouth. When he wanted no more he turned his head aside.

Ben waited until Calahan had also drunk, then suggested that they head back for town. Morrison looked up at Ben and said, "You can kick them crates out and leave 'em. They're about half full of rocks."

Calahan stoppered his canteen and held it in both hands as he stared at Morrison. Ben, too, was staring. Morrison was sweating profusely after taking on a fresh load of water. He flung it off as best he could and looked steadily at Ben. "That's all I know. Them crates was cobbled together at the ranch, hauled up to Henryville north of here and sent down by local freight wagon to the Wileyville corralyard. I know that because I drove the rig up to Henryville and left 'em with the freight company up there."

Ben scowled, but before he could speak Marshal Calahan said, "I told you my sister came runnin' over to tell me you were goin' to take some freight out to the Brittany place. Well, the Brittany's sold this ranch to Jess's paw six, seven years ago. No one's lived here since."

Ben's scowl remained. "Did Job Upton know that?"

"Sure. I expect everyone in the country knew it."

"Then why would Upton tell me the folks out here needed their freight today, and pay me extra to bring it out here?"

Morrison answered and for the first time since he'd been caught, he smiled slightly. "Well now, that ain't too hard to figure out. When we come to town the other day and got into trouble at Joe Benour's saloon, Jess told quite a few folks that he'd sold the Brittany place to some Easterners who were fixin' to move in soon. . . . That was the same day them crates half full of rocks reached town. Jess sent me over to tell Upton the folks who bought the ranch out here wanted their furniture right away an' would pay extra if he got it to them no later than today."

Ben threw up his hands. "I'm having a hell of a time believing all this. If Jess wanted me socked away why didn't he call me out? Or if that notion didn't set well with him, why didn't he—"

Morrison interrupted. "You don't know Jess as well as the marshal and I know him. As far back as I can recollect, he never done anything the quick or sensible way. He's always got to make up some big scheme. His paw used to just listen to Jess and shake his head. Then he'd walk away. I told Jess last night all he had to do to get rid of you was hire someone to shoot you in your bed at the rooming house. There's plenty of men around who'd do that for fifty dollars."

Marshal Calahan cocked an eye at the sky as he asked Morrison where he had left his horse. Morrison jerked his head. "Over yonder maybe half a mile tied in a gully."

They boosted the bushwhacker to his feet and Calahan gave him a rough shove as he said, "Walk, an' keep walkin' until we find your horse."

Ben did not go with them. He rummaged in the freight wagon until he located a prize bar freighters carried to jockey heavy loads around for off-loading, and jackknifed the first crate of "furniture" over the tailgate. When it struck the ground and broke, rocks rolled in all directions.

CHAPTER 17

Not Enough Answers

WHEN Tom Calahan returned with Morrison, who was leading a stocky bay gelding, Ben had dumped the crates and was leaning on the prize bar surveying the wreckage of the boxes and the large jumble of rocks.

Calahan stopped, squinted from the rocks to the bushwhacker and asked if Morrison had helped fill the boxes. Morrison had. "Yeah. We all did. I drove a wagon to a dry creek and that's where we half filled the boxes." Morrison looked at Marshal Calahan. "An' now you're goin' to ask me why in hell Jess wanted that done, an' I'm goin' to tell you I got no idea at all, except that with Jess you can't never make a whole lot of sense of some things he does."

Calahan picked up several of the rocks, examined them, turned them over and shot Morrison a look. The bushwhacker rolled his eyes. "Your guess is as good as mine. I already told you, I got no idea what Jess had in mind."

Calahan tossed the rocks aside, left Morrison with Ben while he went to the shoeing shed for his horse, and during his absence Morrison asked Moore if he knew how the lawman had known Morrison was going to be out there waiting.

Ben could only say that if the bushwhacker wanted the answer to that question he should ask the marshal. Morrison turned his back and recinched his horse, which bore the Hearst brand on its left shoulder. Ben said, "What's a life worth to you?"

Morrison answered without even looking away from his work. "Fifty dollars an' a good horse to leave the country on." He dropped the stirrup leather and turned. "But there's somethin' goin' on an' if I'd known it last night I wouldn't have hired on to put you away."

"What makes you think something is going on? Like what?"

Morrison looked over his shoulder as Marshal Calahan was crossing the yard, then turned back as he said, "I don't know. Something, though. Couple days back I was gathering the remuda to bring it in to replace the horses we been usin' and they was a hell of a distance off, but I'd swear I seen Jess talkin' to a couple of fellers."

"His riders?" asked Ben.

Morrison shook his head. "No. All the riders was back in the yard except me—and Jess."

Marshal Calahan came up, snugged up, turned his horse without speaking and swung up across leather, then looked at the two men on the ground and waited. Ben climbed to the wagon seat and lined out the big draft animals. Calahan and Morrison rode behind the tailgate for a while, then rode up ahead. Ben could not hear what they said, but it was not much. Marshal Calahan did not seem to be in a talkative mood. Several times he sat sideways looking back, not at the wagon, but back in the direction of the old ranch yard.

Ben was killing time, trying to fit odd bits together. All he could come up with was that either Job Upton had known Jess Hearst wanted Ben Moore in the Brittany ranch yard and had seen to it that this happened, or Jeff Hoffman's quitting was not the result of all his complaining and threats over the past few years.

If he were correct in either case it still added up to someone deliberately sending Ben out into the country to be killed. That Marshal Calahan had either known or suspected there was a plot to kill Ben he did not question. Otherwise Calahan would hardly have appeared as he did, looking for, and finding, a bushwhacker.

Ben watched the pair of riders up ahead, let his lines lie slack because the big horses were as dutifully keeping the wagon in the ruts on the return trip as they had on the trip coming out and relaxed against the back of the spring-seat.

If Marshal Calahan did not pick up the gait they were not going to reach town by supper time. Ben was recalling what Calahan had said about his sister running over to the jail-house when Ben told her where he was going with the wagon, when it struck him that Morrison was right about one thing. Something sure as hell was going on, and the more Ben speculated, the less sense he could make of it.

Both the Calahans must either know about or have suspicions of whatever was behind all this. He could not imagine what it might be, but he felt certain that Jess Hearst was implicated up to his eyes.

There were diagonal high, thin clouds patterning the late-day sky with a red, lowering sun shooting rays of rusty gold over the bottoms of the clouds, making a kind of lattice design.

Morrison, the non-contrite, matter-of-fact bushwhacker, was discussing something with Marshal Calahan, who appeared to be listening as he slouched in his saddle. Ben was watching them when he saw movement dead ahead and slightly to the west, which was in the direction of one of those arroyos of which this more southerly range appeared to have its share.

Ben said nothing. He did not move. He watched for a repitition of whatever had attracted his attention and although he was absolutely certain he had seen *something,* too many years of being surprised by furtive four-legged creatures induced him to suspect that this was what he had seen this time. Probably an old gummer coyote.

Ben was bone-tired. It had been a long day, and it was not over yet. Nothing had really turned out as he'd had every right to think it should when he arose this morning.

His gaze flicked to Tom Calahan, who was twisting to look back. When their eyes met, Ben made a crooked smile and the lawman returned the gesture.

"I don't think it was Upton," Calahan said. "And Morrison has been tellin' me where they went to put rocks in those crates."

"Yeah," Ben replied. "They went to a creek bed. He already told us that. Or maybe you were over after your horse and didn't hear."

Instead of facing forward, Calahan placed one big gloved hand upon the rump of his horse behind the cantle and eyed Ben Moore. "Yeah. I knew about the creek bed. . . . Tell me something; has anyone showed you the section corners of the old Oakley place?"

"No. Who would be around to do that? If the lads know, they never mentioned it. Anyway, what's important about that?"

Calahan's black eyes were fixed on Moore now. "Well, now, I got to assume you don't know where the borders are of your neighbor's land either, because if you knew one, you'd know the other."

Ben shifted his attention to the arroyo to the west where he had seen that earlier movement, then shifted his gaze back to Calahan. "Are you tryin' to tell me something?" he asked a trifle ruefully.

Calahan's thin mouth pulled wide in an effigy of a smile. "Yeah. That arrowhead the lad gave you . . ."

"What of it?"

"It came from the same creek bed as the rocks you dumped out of those boxes back yonder."

Ben continued to eye the lawman. "If this is supposed to be an explanation, Marshal, it's a sorry excuse for one."

Suddenly there was just a gunshot—not particularly loud and lacking much of an aftermath echo, but evidently it accompished its purpose. Before Marshal Calahan and Ben Moore could straighten up in shock, the burly bushwhacker was already falling.

Morrison went down the near side of his horse, feet free, and although he struck the ground solidly enough to startle some horses, Morrison's own animal simply side-stepped, went ahead another yard or so, halted and swung its head to look back. The solid weight of the man who had been riding the horse had undoubtedly surprised the animal by no longer being up there. Otherwise the horse was indifferent.

Marshal Calahan's recovery was swift. He had palmed his six-gun before straightening fully around. There was a faint hint of soiled gunsmoke in the westerly distance. As he was raising his rein hand, he asked if Ben had seen the gunman. Ben had not but he knew burnt gunpowder when he saw it, and he pointed.

Calahan put his horse into a lope, heading for the distant arroyo. Ben Moore watched him while shaking his head and muttering to himself: a man did not have to be brave to do what Tom Calahan was doing—charging straight into the gun range of someone who had already proved himself very capable with sighted weapons—he had to be foolish. Ben held his breath but there was no second gunshot, not in Calahan's direction or in any other direction.

Ben felt chilled by that, too. Whoever had shot Morrison had in all probability not done it by mistake. Ben swung to the ground, dropped a tether weight, scuffed up where Morrison was lying on his back and sank down to study the wound. It was not bleeding because the bullet had passed through within an inch of the dead man's heart.

Ben raised up, spat, looked around, saw no sign of Marshal Calahan and stood up. It did not make much difference about Morrison; he wasn't going anywhere. But Ben was worrying about Elizabeth's brother. There was no sign of him. There ws no sign of anyone else either. Ben cursed, hauled the dead bushwhacker's mount around, ran two fingers beneath the cinch, swung up and reined in the direction of the arroyo.

Behind him, the big harness horses watched with stolid lack of particular concern for a while, then yanked their heads for slack and leaned to lip at whatever they could find that was edible.

The arroyo had heat down in it. It was also humid because the footing was marshy in places with flourishing under-growth growing in knee-high tangles. Ben rode with his gun in his lap behind the swells and out of sight. He relied on the horse more than upon himself, which proved to be wise. The horse made a sideways swipe at some tall stalks, got them properly positioned with its powerful grinders and bore down, cutting through coarse grass as though it were bone-dry. But before the animal got ready to begin masticating he suddenly sucked back and with a snort lowered his head.

The movement was so abrupt, violent and unexpected that Ben was barely able to catch himself. Marshal Calahan's animal was standing like a statue watching Ben's horse and did not move, even after Moore had swung to the ground and shouldered past the inert animal to make certain his worst misgiving was accurate. Marshal Calahan was lying there in tangled ripgut as limp as a rag, with blood on his shirt, his hat gone and his breathing shallow and labored.

But Ben had not heard the gunshot.

As Ben put up his Colt and knelt to examine the lawman, a quiet, flat voice spoke from the underbrush to his right. "Just don't move. . . . Not even your eyes. . . . I always like seein' a man already in a prayin' position."

Ben was less surprised that he had been caught hands-down than that he was positive he had recognized the voice from the underbrush. But he obeyed; he neither raised his head nor made a sound.

The unseen spokesman raised his voice slightly, address-ing someone else. "This here is the one. Look close an' you'll see I'm right."

For a while there was no reply. When it came it was in a gruff, growly tone. "All right. It don't make no difference anyway."

"Yeah, it does," the other man replied. "That one you hit

in the back of the head with the rock is the town marshal of Wileyville."

"What the hell of it?"

"They'll expect him back."

The growly-voiced man stepped from an area of shaggy little trees and thornpin thicket, hooked his thumbs and gazed at Ben Moore's back. "Go over this one," he said, and gave Ben an order. "Stand up, cowboy. Drop the gun and keep your back to me. . . . All right, Pete. Search him."

When Pete Bruno approached Ben and their eyes met, Pete's expression showed no embarrassment. He smiled as he spoke. "You look almighty puzzled," he said and halted a yard away. "I don't blame you—you bein' new hereabouts and all."

Ben took a chance and blew out a resigned breath as he said, "What in the hell is this about, Pete? You're still with Hearst?"

"Never wasn't with him, cowboy. . . . Empty your pockets."

Ben obediently dropped his possessions to the ground, but as he did so he continued to eye Pete Bruno. Finally he said, "You're a disappointment to me, Pete."

Bruno ignored that and said to the growly-voiced man back in the shadows behind Ben Moore, "Come see for yourself. . . . I told you he didn't know anything."

The gruff man shambled around until Ben could see his profile as the unkempt individual leaned to poke with a boot toe among Ben's personal belongings on the ground. Ben knew this man too, but knowing him did not help much. He said, "Jeff, just to satisfy my damned ignorance—tell me what the hell this is all about."

Jeff Hoffman, that chronically complaining freight and stage driver for Job Upton in Wileyville, turned a sullen glare upon Ben, pointed with a rigid brown finger at the things in the grass and said, "Where is it?" He raised the finger slowly and aimed it directly at Ben's chest as though it were a gun barrel.

Ben glanced down, then up. "Where is what?" He made a bewildered, flapping gesture with both arms. "I didn't believe it from the start," Bruno said. "I told Jess it didn't sound right. . . . I might as well have been arguin' with a damned tree."

This last remark hit Ben hard. He stared at Pete. "Morrison saw Jess talkin' to a pair of men out on the range. . . . Pete, that was you and Jeff."

Bruno eyed Ben with his head slightly to one side for a moment, then said, "You're not as thick as I thought, cowboy."

None of this had distracted Jeff Hoffman, who was fishing in a filthy old pocket for a plug of chewing tobacco, which he gnawed on as he fixed Ben with a merciless stare and said, "You listen to me, cowboy. Morrison was supposed to get it off your carcass. We was watchin' from out here to see if he got it. An' if he did, we was to take it from him and give it to Jess. . . .He didn't get it. Now I'm goin' to blow your brains out whether you tell me what you done with it or not." As he finished speaking, Jeff pulled out an old rebuilt cavalry pistol that had been originally chambered for hand loading.

Bruno interrupted with a frantic gesture. "Damn it, suppose he give it to the lawman? I told you, Jeff, when we saw him stalkin' Morrison, Marshal Calahan bein' out here wasn't no damned accident. He had to know something. . . . Well, search him. Go on, search him. If he don't have it, you can overhaul this one. . . . Jeff, for Christ's sake we ain't got all day. *Search him!*"

CHAPTER 18

A Climax

THE disreputable teamster spat, eyed Bruno and Ben in turn, then knelt and began tearing at the pockets of the wounded lawman. Ben watched, as did Pete Bruno, but Ben's curiosity was greater than his interest. Whatever these men were after certainly had significance; even bushwhackers did not shoot people for target practice.

Hoffman finished on the ground and rocked back, glaring upward. "Cowboy, I told you, I'm goin' to bust your head like a punky melon. *Where is it?!*"

Pete Bruno looked disgustedly at the seamy old stained teamster. "Sometimes you don't make any sense at all, Jeff. It's not on him and shootin' him isn't goin' to find it. If we go back without it, we both lose fifty dollars."

Hoffman grunted up to his feet, glaring. "All right, you're so smart, you find it."

Ben turned his back on the teamster, facing Bruno. "You said I don't have it. Old greasy here says the marshal don't have it. I'm a trader, Pete. You tell me what we're lookin' for, and I'll tell you straight out if I know anything about it."

Before Hoffman could snarl, Bruno said, "A arrowhead, pretty fair-sized one. Sort of mealy-looking, not black obsidian or redstone."

Ben looked steadily at the rangeman. "Arrowhead. You killed a man and hit another one over the head with a rock for a damned arrowhead?"

Bruno spoke shortly. "Where is it? You made the offer, we taken you up on it. Now, where is it?"

"I don't know where it is, and that's the gospel truth, so help me. I was told to bring some crates out here and—"

138

"Ah hell," snarled the teamster. "We know all that. I'm not goin' to listen to it again, neither." Hoffman was dragging out his old re-bored handgun when Ben turned on him.

He glared at Jeff Hoffman and said, "Arrowhead. You're crazy, Hoffman. I don't own an arrowhead and shootin' me isn't goin' to get it for you. What in the hell is important about a darned arrowhead?"

Hoffman held the gun in its holster as he eyed Moore. He seemed to be genuinely frustrated. It was Bruno who answered the question. "There's two of 'em. Jess already has the one that old Fred Oakley lost to him in a poker game last winter. Half the map is scratched on it. He's got to have the other one to make 'em fit."

Ben turned slowly to eye Hoffman. The older man said, "I seen the one Jess has. The scratching on the top is some sort of continuation that when a man butts the second arrowhead to it completes the drawing."

"What drawing?" Ben asked and saw the inert man on the ground flex one leg very faintly. He looked away from that and repeated the question. "What drawing?"

Pete Bruno answered. "A map. Jess said it most likely was out yonder where we went and chucked rocks into them crates you brought out here. . . . But it wasn't out there. We kicked rocks and punched holes until the cows come home. Never found it."

Ben raised an arm to shove his hat back, but neither of his companions interpreted that movement as a threat. They simply stood there looking at him until he asked another question.

"A map scratched on a pair of Indian arrowheads, and Jess needs the other. . . . Are you sayin' there's somethin' buried somewhere up north and those arrowheads are the key to finding it?"

Bruno nodded, shot Hoffman a quizzical look, then spoke almost wearily. "Indian loot from raidin' down into Mexico. Jess's been hearin' that story since he was a child. Even his old paw knew about it. Only he didn't know where the cache was. All anyone seemed to know was there had to be another of them mealy-lookin' arrowpoints to lead the way to the cache. Then there was that poker session an' it turned up that if old Fred knew anything, he went and taken that damned arrowpoint with him when he left the country. In fact Jess believes that's why old Fred left. To keep from maybe havin' the soles burnt off his feet to make him tell."

Ben remembered something. "That place you fellers filled the crates with rocks—you thought that was where the cache was buried?"

"Yeah. It's got to be somewhere. Don't any of us really care where, just as long as we find it before the snow flies."

Hoffman the teamster got busy scratching an itch inside his shirt, then he said, "I knew you didn't have that damned thing." He was almost casually conversational, as though they were friends, and it was entirely possible that, like the dead bushwhacker, his interest was not based on anything except doing a job.

Of one thing Ben felt assured: Bruno had talked the teamster out of doing something rash. Ben could have been thankful for that, but the opportunity did not arise. With two savage kicks from the ground, Marshal Calahan caught Hoffman behind both legs, hurtling him forward where he collided with an astonished Pete Bruno, grabbing the rider as he struggled to maintain his balance. Ben pivoted lightly, hit Bruno under the left ear with a gloved fist, and as Bruno turned loose, Ben caught Hoffman, whirled him and struck him twice, very hard.

Marshal Calahan sat up, eyed the pair of downed men, held up an arm and groaned. Ben hoisted him to his feet. Calahan felt the sticky back of his head, wobbled and looked for something to lean on. He was dirty, bloody and gray-looking, but the expression in his dark eyes was murderous when he considered Hoffman and Bruno. Ben stood working his gloved hands. He had used them both like mauls. They were painful but most noticeable, they were swelling.

He and Calahan regarded each other. When the taciturn lawman said nothing Ben spoke. "Did you hear what they said about some arrowheads?"

Calahan had. "Yeah. I've heard the story fifty times. Never believed any of it until you said you was to fetch some crates out to the old ranch today. Then I remembered seein' them fillin' those crates near the Hearst property line next to the Oakley place." Calahan straightened up, accepted his six-gun from Moore and leathered it, looking down again. His dark gaze fixed on Moore. "I'll tell you what I thought. Jess figured you most likely didn't just happen into the country. Specially after you taken up at the Oakley place. Sure as hell, he suspected you were after his damned cache. So he paid Jeff to quit Upton, schemed to get you to haul the crates out here and figured to overhaul you, kill you if necessary, to find out what you knew. . . . So I snuck out here too."

As Calahan finished speaking, he gingerly felt his bruise again, regarded the blood on his fingers and swore. "Morrison's dead?"

"Like a stone."

"No loss. I'd like you to answer a question for me."

"Shoot."

"You really won that ranch from the old man?"

"Yes. Up north."

"An' he never mentioned anything about a cache, some old arrowheads, anything like that?"

"He didn't say fifteen words. Later, when I went lookin' for him he was gone, an' the weather was building up, so I left. That's everything I know."

Ben eyed the sprawled men on the ground. "What do you want to do with them?"

"Take 'em back, lock 'em up, and after that it'll be up to them. Bruno, well, he's just another drifting saddle-tramp, but Jeff Hoffman is a worthless, whining old everlastin'

schemer. I've had him in and out of my cells a dozen times.
. . . He'd have killed you sure as hell. Probably me too. You
want to drive the wagon over here so's we can load them up
and get back to town?"

Ben nodded.

By the time Ben got back to the arroyo Marshal Calahan
had both their prisoners standing up, looking glum. None of
them said a word as the prisoners climbed atop their animals,
whose shanks were tied to the tailgate of the wagon. From up
there both Bruno and Hoffman could see the dead bushwhacker, face down in the wagon bed.

Dusk was settling by the time they had Wileyville in sight.
There hadn't been twenty words spoken on the entire trip
back, but that did not imply there was not some serious
thinking going on, at least with Ben Moore.

His view of a possible cache was tempered by the lawman's
skepticism. On the other hand he knew where that second
arrowhead was. Or at least he remembered Jamie having it
the only time Ben saw the thing.

What appeared to rank in importance now was not to let
anyone know Jamie had the arrowhead—and to get his hands
on the one Jess Hearst had. That, he told himself as he
straightened up on the seat as they came to the lower end of
town, was likely to require something besides a simple re-
quest.

He helped unload the dead man and both prisoners in the
alley behind the jailhouse, then tooled the rig up to Upton's
yard, where there was no one around, so he cared for the
animals by himself, left the rig in the center of the yard and
went back to the wash-rack to clean up. He was hungry, but
not to the exclusion of some bothersome thoughts, so instead
of heading for the café he hiked up to the doctor's place and
met Elizabeth on the porch. She looked a little quizzical as
she asked if anything had happened that afternoon. He told
her bluntly about her brother's injury, the dead man and the
prisoners. She held a hand to her throat until he was fin-

ished, then hurried southward in the direction of the lighted jailhouse.

Ben entered the Pittinger house, met no one in the parlor but heard voices out back and went through to the kitchen.

Jamie and Doctor Pittinger were playing cards and both looked up in complete surprise. Ben sank into a chair, winked at Jamie and accepted a cup of black java from the medical practitioner. He told his story again, and as before, omitted any mention of arrowheads. Doc Pittinger's professional interest was in the dead man, and more urgently, the injured marshal. He left the house clutching his black satchel.

Ben regarded the elder Oakley boy owlishly when he asked about young Arthur. Jamie smiled. "Sleeps mostly, but Miz Elizabeth gets him to eat. Puny though, weaker'n a cat."

"What's Doc say?"

"Says maybe by next week he can go back with us to the ranch."

Ben pushed aside the emptied coffee cup and placed his hand palm-up atop the table. "Let me see the arrowhead," he said.

Jamie produced it from a trouser pocket and watched Ben hold it to the lamp examining it closely. When Ben lowered his hand to the tabletop Jamie said, "Pretty big for an arrowhead, ain't it? I told Arthur it maybe was more like a hunting head Indians wedged into long sticks, like a lance."

Ben flaked at the arrowhead with a broken thumbnail and said nothing until he was holding the point to the light again. There were faint but discernible scratchings on it. He looked at Jamie. "You know exactly where Arthur found this thing?"

For a moment Ben's heart sank because Jamie did not speak. Then the boy said, "Yeah, I know. In that thicket where we been living. Way deep in there. There is a sort of sunken place. That's where he found the arrowhead. I was there an' saw him pick it up."

Ben was staring. "Sunken place? Like maybe someone had dug there?"

Jamie was not sure. "Maybe, only we figured it was one of them wallows critters make to scratch in."

Ben eyed the arrowhead, then placed it atop the table. If someone had been digging where the boys had found the arrowhead, there was a good chance the arrowhead had been pitched aside after someone had found the cache—if there ever was a cache. Ben suddenly thought of the silent old man he had played poker with.

Doctor Pittinger returned with Elizabeth. They brought a draft of cool night air in with them. Doc nodded as he said, "You've been busy," to Ben and went over to the stove for coffee.

Elizabeth sank down at the table without a word. For a while the only sound was of coffee being poured, then Jamie left the room to go see his brother and Elizabeth raised her very dark eyes to Ben's face. "I knew it had to be something like that. Otherwise there'd be no reason for you to go out there with a wagon."

Ben shrugged. "I guess I should say I'm glad you sent your brother along. But why send me out there with those darned rocks? Why not just empty boxes?"

She smiled as though he were a child. "Empty boxes don't weigh as much as loaded ones. You were supposed to believe you were hauling freight."

She picked up the arrowhead, turned it gently and put it down, showing no particular interest in it. Unless it was held directly to the light, those faint scratches did not show. Doctor Pittinger joined them at the table. He too eyed the arrowhead, but paid no attention. "Which one of them shot Morrison?" he asked, over the lip of his cup.

Ben frowned. "Didn't they tell the marshal?"

"No. They said neither of them did it. And that's got to be a lie."

Ben gazed steadily at the older man. "Marshal Calahan had their six-guns."

Pittinger shrugged. "Hadn't been fired. Neither of them."

Ben's jaw sagged. He looked from Pittinger to Calahan's sister—and the hair along the back of his neck stood up. Someone sure as hell had killed Morrison with a long shot from that darned arroyo. He rubbed his jaw. Had there been *three* men out there? If so, why hadn't the third one walked out when the fight started?

Elizabeth leaned to tap Ben's arm. "You look starved. Come down to the café with me."

He arose, pocketed the arrowhead and looked at Pittinger, who seemed to be somewhere else in thought as he nodded to them, and who, as Elizabeth led the way back through the house to the roadway, heaved a rattling big sigh, shoved up to his feet and went trooping through the house in the direction of the room where young Arthur and his brother were.

CHAPTER 19

Calahan's Resolve

MARSHALL Calahan entered the lighted café, locked the door after himself, sat at the counter wearing a clean shirt and a tidy bandage. His sister brought him broth. He grinned at her.

"You're trouble," he told her, and she ignored the remark.

"Are you sure neither of their guns had been fired, Tom?"

"Plumb sure, Liz. Only I didn't know it until we got back to town an' I sat down to examine them." His black eyes were fixed on her face.

Ben cut in. "All right. Where was the third man?"

Calahan noisily sipped broth before replying. "Gone. I'll go back out there in the morning to find his tracks, but Hoffman an' Pete said—"

"Oh, hell," exclaimed Ben Moore irritably. "He shot Morrison. I saw the smoke comin' up out of that arroyo. Bruno and Hoffman had to know he was there. They had to have heard the gunshot. Hell, you and I were a lot farther off an' we heard it."

Calahan did not argue. He finished his broth, waited until Elizabeth had brought a refill, then he said, "Ben, I like your company. It's a little hard on my carcass, and settin' here talkin isn't going to get us anywhere. First off, I'll bet my badge I know who shot Morrison. I don't know exactly why, except that in messes like this, folks get in the habit of shootin' first and thinkin' second."

Ben's exasperation had not passed. He stared at Calahan. "Marshal, those two gents in your cells got to know more than they've let on. Hell, no one walks up behind you in a

146

damned arroyo, shoots someone, then rides away without you seeing *something*."

Tom Calahan started on his second large bowl of hot beef broth before speaking again. He put the cup down and looked straight at Ben Moore. "I don't think you're a very good liar," he said dispassionately, "about that confounded arrowhead."

Ben glared. "The hell with the arrowhead. There's someone loping around here killin' people—me next or maybe you."

Calahan shoved the empty cup aside nodding his head. "All right. For now forget the arrowhead . . . How do you feel?"

"How do I—?"

"This time I'm not goin' to ride blind."

"Ride where?"

"To the Hearst ranch. Tonight."

Elizabeth stared at her brother. "Tom, he has six riders out there."

"Naw. Unless he's hired more men he's only got three left. Morrison, Bruno and Hoffman are out of it."

"Hoffman didn't ride for him, Tom."

"Then He's got four men. Maybe. Liz, it's my nature to keep goin' when I get hold of something. Night or day. I'm goin' out there tonight. With Ben or —"

Someone rattled the roadside door fiercely. Ben jumped and the lawman swung on the bench. Elizabeth recognized the silhouette as belonging to a large man. Tall rather than thick. She went to the door, unlocked it and the unsmiling lanky saloon owner walked in. Joe Benour eyed the three of them for a silent moment, then approached the counter and tossed something atop it.

"Saw you in here," he told Marshal Calahan. "This afternoon two riders I never seen before came in for drinks. They was interested in folks around town. One of them dropped this on the floor when he was fishin' in a pants pocket to pay up. . . . You know what that is, Marshal?"

Calahan knew. "It's a gold double eagle."

Benour pursed his lips, ignored Ben and Elizabeth and scowled at the lawman. "You know who used to pay with those things?"

Calahan palmed the coin. It was worn. He looked up at the barman. "The old man. Charley Hearst. That was his trademark. He told me a dozen times he had no faith in silver or paper money. . . . Joe?"

Benour finally looked at Elizabeth and Ben Moore. He knew about the killing and about the two prisoners at the town jailhouse. In a place like Wileyville, news traveled quick as lightning. Particularly news about someone being killed. "Those two saddle-tramps bought grub at the emporium and left town. Marshal, do you know what they were up to?"

"I can guess," replied Calahan, arising, handing Benour the gold coin. "I need a couple of possemen, Joe."

Benour nodded woodenly. "All right. You can explain what the hell is goin' on as we ride. . . . Now then, where are we going?"

"To the Hearst place."

Benour was perfectly agreeable. "Then let's go." He gazed at the handsome woman and she gazed back. "How are the little boys, ma'am?"

"Coming right along."

"Fine. I got deep-down reasons for wanting to pay someone back for bein' hard on little kids. Marshal, I also never had any use for Jess Hearst. . . . Just you'n me and Mister Moore?"

Elizabeth seemed about to speak when her brother arose and jerked his head for Ben to join them on their way out of the café. At the door Ben looked back. She had both hands gripped across the front of her apron. He smiled at her. "I want to give you something." He went back and handed her the arrowhead. "Keep it. I'll explain later."

"You be careful out there," she said, then looked swiftly away. "Tom, all three of you be careful out there."

Marshal Calahan opened the door, closed it after the three men were outside, then wagged his head until pain made him stop it.

The night was bell-clear with every star pegged exactly in place. It was getting cold. By morning there was going to be a thick rind of white frost on troughs and treetops.

Calahan told Joe Benour all he knew, suspected, or was worrying about as they rode out of town. Benour listened quietly; he rode straight up in the saddle, like a man with a ramrod up his back. Beneath his broadcloth Prince Albert coat, he was armed and ready.

An hour later Benour said, "Tom . . . that damned arrow-head-cache yarn has been around since I was in three-cornered britches."

Calahan was peering into the oncoming dark as he dryly replied. "Yeah. So has the yarn about Noah's ark. What's that prove—that there wasn't one?"

This was as far off the Oakley place as Ben had been since he came to Wileyville. They left the roadbed and loped overland on a slightly northwesterly course. After a couple of hours Marshal Calahan drew rein once, listened to the night the way a man might do who knew he was close enough to something that made sounds to listen for it, then he turned toward Ben Moore.

"What'd you give Liz?" he asked in his blunt manner.

Ben aswered the same way. "An old arrowhead."

Benour stopped too. Both local men looked steadily at Ben, then Benour said, "Are you goin' to tell me that legend about an Indian cache is true?"

Ben smiled to take the sting out of his words. "I'm not going to tell you a damned thing, except that if we sit out here talkin' the night away, I'd just as soon go back to the rooming house."

Joe Benour did not look happy with that response, and as

he and Marshal Calahan led off again, Benour turned twice to stare at Ben Moore. Neither time did he open his mouth.

A little ground-swell wind came hastening southward from some cold mountains. It made grass heads bend and sway, then it passed, and into the ensuing silence a cow bawled somewhere ahead and to the east. She bawled three times, each time more insistently.

Ben knew the sound. Her calf had his belly full of warm milk, was bedded down somewhere out of the cold wind, and whether he heard her or not, he would give no sign of it until he was darned good and ready, which probably meant about dawn, when he'd be hungry again.

The horses picked up the smoke fragrance their riders could not discern for some time afterward. The second time Calahan stopped, he leaned with both gloved hands atop the saddle horn looking into the yonder night. Ben's impression about this was that Calahan knew exactly where they were, and exactly where something like a ranch yard was.

Benour quietly said, "What's it feel like?"

Calahan's reply was short. "Can't be sure. I don't know. There's four men and Jess. Unless those two who lost the double eagle in your place are out here too."

Joe Benour was largely a blank space to Ben Moore, except that Ben had made a roughed-out sort of cursory appraisal of the tall man that left him suspecting the saloon proprietor would not be a good individual to cross. Those casual remarks about children being abused provided Ben with the basis for his other feeling about Benour: the saloon proprietor had a store of hatred in his heart—let Joe Benour be convinced someone had deliberately shot at two little boys and was trying to dispossess them, and according to Moore's instinct, the saloonman would show no mercy.

He did not look like a merciful individual as he sat on his horse, coat buttoned, hat pulled low, waiting for Tom Calahan to take the initiative.

The marshal gestured for Moore's benefit. "Up ahead

maybe a mile." Calahan lowered his arm. "It's a big yard. You stay close to Joe an' me. . . . Joe, if there's lights at the bunkhouse . . . "

Benour nodded stiffly, and Ben was surprised when moonlight showed a smile on his stony features. "Someday I'll tell you a story, Tom."

That was all Benour said, but the words and the tone of voice were pretty convincing. Then he twisted to glance at Ben. "You haven't said ten words. What's your interest, Mister Moore?"

"My name is Ben. Not Mister Moore. My interest is in that arrowhead Hearst has. I figure after what he's done to the boys, then to me, he owes us that much."

"And then what?"

Ben flared back. "How the hell do I know?"

Benour took the sharp rebuke still smiling and winked at Marshal Calahan. They rode a hundred yards before a dog began furiously barking. Ben flinched but neither of his companions did; dogs barked. In this kind of country barking dogs could mean wolves were on the prowl or maybe a foraging band of coyotes was looking for a calving ground where they could glean afterbirth. Or it could simply mean timid deer were following the scent of curing feed.

It could also mean two-legged trouble.

The lights were yellow rather than white. There were three sets of them; one on the west side of the big old tree-marked yard coming from a small window in a square log bunkhouse. The farthest southward window glowed from what eventually became visible as the Hearst ranch's main house, residence of the owner.

The final lighted window was on their left. which was to the east as they came down to the edge of the yard from the north. That building was long, with a covered big porch and no tie racks. It was the cookhouse. The *cocinero* was probably sitting in there in his stocking feet, sipping laced java and reading an old newspaper, if he could read—otherwise he might be thumbing through a saddle and harness catalog. A man didn't have to know how to read; rigging catalogs were abundantly illustrated.

Calahan knew this place as well as he knew the back of his hand, and he led them around behind the mightly old log barn, where a corralful of using horses came up to lean on the stringers and watch them dismount.

The marshal lifted his hat and reset it, probably without being conscious of doing it. He waited until their animals had been made fast to stud-rings in the rear outside logs of the barn, then said, "Joe . . . ?"

Benour nodded, loosened his black coat all the way down and with his face in the direction of the lighted bunkhouse simple strode away from his companions. After he was little more than a faint-swaying blend of lighter darkness up ahead, Tom Calahan sighed and said, "That story he said he'd tell me sometime . . . Nine years ago in Jackson Hole he rode up to a log house in the dead of winter, left his horse in some trees and with a sawed-off shotgun blew the door off the cabin with his first blast and killed three horse thieves at their supper table with the second blast."

Ben said nothing. He was not surprised. As the angular dark silhouette faded from sight near the small covered front porch of the bunkhouse, Ben shook his head. "No shotgun this time, Marshal."

Calahan had already passed this point and was studying the distant main house. The barking dog was over there somewhere, still furiously caterwauling. Generally, people did not worry much about a dog barking in a ranch yard at night. Generally. But this time maybe someone would because, for a damned fact, by now Jess Hearst knew he was shy two hired riders and a bribed teamster.

The marshal led the way by remaining on the west side of the yard, where outbuildings of various size gave adequate cover most of the way to the immediate vicinity of Jess Hearst's big old sprawling ranch home.

Calahan stopped so suddenly Ben bumped him. The dog had finally got someone's curiosity aroused. A door opened, dumping an elongated glow of lamplight down across the porch, where it was diffused near the main house hitch rack. The man who was up there on the porch was no novice; he was moving away from backgrounding light even before Ben and Tom caught much more than a glimpse of him.

Ben leaned to whisper, "That wasn't Hearst. He wasn't big enough."

Calahan was like stone. He did not indicate that he had heard a word of Ben's remark. The man on the porch was remaining back along the front of the house, away from the only window in the front wall. They knew he was up there, maybe straining to hear or trying to see something. They scarcely breathed while they waited.

When the dog finally stopped barking, probably because he was satisfied at having roused someone, a faint sound of laughter came from the direction of the lighted bunkhouse, where smoke was rising lazily from the mud-wattle chimney.

Ben said, softly, "Poker game."

Calahan nodded and finally responded vocally. "Can you make him out? Is he still standin' back there along the wall?"

Moore scowled hard in an effort to see better and had to give it up. "I don't see anything, but then he wouldn't be figuring to let me anyway. He's either still up there on the porch or he's gone off it somewhere, maybe to the east, and might be skulkin' around the yard."

CHAPTER 20

Confusion

THE idea of the stalkers being stalked held Calahan stone-still for a while. The moon was moving, the field of stars glowed, and a high, vagrant breeze that had just about exhaused its momentum carried the hauntingly sad, very distant sound of a wolf.

Ben brushed his companion's arm. "We can split up."

Calahan was as still as a rock when he replied so quietly Ben had to strain to catch the words. "Get closer to the shadows of this here shed. Now then—skyline the east side, over near the cookshack. See anything?"

Ben took his time replying. "Yeah. But he don't act like he's stalking. He's going over there behind the shoeing shed in the direction of the cookshack."

The Marshal remained silent. They watched the silhouette. It came and went, moved through sooty shadows and out again into pewter moonlight. Calahan did not speculate. As he had said back at the café, he was inclined toward action, not conjecture. He gestured with his left hand. "Let him get inside, then you go north around to the upper end, cross over and come down behind the cookhouse. I'll go southward and get over there too. Wait for me out back."

Moore turned back the way they had come, passed the lined-up horses along the corral fence who watched him with the identical curiosity they had demonstrated earlier. But they did not make a sound.

He went far out and around their own tethered animals to avoid being nickered at, reached the upper end of the yard, waited until he was entirely satisfied that unless someone was

154

very close they would not see him cross to the east, then moved out.

He was standing in wall shadow north of the cookshack when a man came out onto the rear porch, heaved dregs from a large old blueware pot and went back inside. Moore had only a few moments to see this man, and because he had a respectable paunch hanging over his britches and belt, Ben was confident this one was the ranch cook.

If he was going to brew up fresh java this late at night, he was probably only hastening an operation he would ordinarily not have to bother with until dawn light. So whoever that silhouette had belonged to was probably inside with the cook.

Ben took his time getting down to the back of the cookshack because he thought Marshal Calahan would require even more time. He was wrong; Calahan was waiting, looking impatient and testy. Ben moved silently close, mentioned the cook dumping his coffee dregs, and Marshal Calahan cut across that explanation as though coffee grounds were absolutely the farthest thing from his mind, which they were.

"Awright. There's two in there. Possum-belly and the gent we been watching. There are two doors. One from out front, one from out back. Which one do you want?"

Ben was eyeing the rough plank wall as he answered. "What difference does that make? We can both go in through the rear door. If they're having some coffee at the table they're not goin' to get away."

Calahan's annoyed expression deepened. "Remind me never to use a posseman again. Suppose we go in back and they are going out the front?"

Ben said, "All right. I'll take the front door. . . . Listen— there's voices across the yard."

He was correct, but they were not very menacing voices, even after a man who had just returned from peeing out back rather breathlessly reported seeing tethered saddled animals behind the barn.

After that the men at the bunkhouse did not say a word,

or if they did, Calahan and Moore did not hear it. Inside the cookshack the sound of someone snapping kindling wood carried as though the man doing this was right out there with the marshal and his companion.

Calahan was getting perturbed. Having their horses found promised no good. He jerked his head, drew his handgun and headed for the rear cookshack door. As he was doing this, Ben Moore went in the opposite direction. Toward the front door.

It would occur to Ben Moore much later that if Calahan had been a little more circumspect they would not have left their saddle animals where somenone might stumble onto them. If this amounted to a mistake, it was probably due to the same blind spot mounted men had since Year One—they rode as far as they could, then they walked.

Ben was holding his six-gun in one hand, reaching for the doorlatch with the other hand, when what sounded like a mule kicking an oak barrel sent a tearing sound through the night.

Ben slammed open his door and crab-crouched into the lighted cookshack. He might as well have been invisible. There were two men seated at a long scarred old cookhouse dining table holding crockery coffee mugs in both hands, with their upper bodies and heads turned toward the back of the big room where Marshall Calahan was standing wide-legged in the opening where a mighty kick had broken the rear door from its lower hinge.

There was absolutely no motion for seconds. The startled coffee-drinkers required time to gather fragmented thoughts, and Tom Calahan needed about the same length of time to adjust. It had been dark outside. Inside it was lamplight-bright.

Ben cocked his six-gun; the sound cut into the rapidly diminishing echoes of the rear door being kicked loose. A large beard-straggled heavy man who looked unkempt and swarthy turned his head slowly. He was in stocking feet and was not wearing a weapon. The man opposite him was younger, beefy through the upper body, but not fat, and this man was armed, but as he started to face the sound of the cocked gun Marshal Calahan said, "Sit still. Keep your hands atop the table." Calahan shifted his aimed gun from the swarthy, graying man to the stranger as he said; "Ben, disarm him."

Ben moved in without haste. There was no opposition, although now the astonishment was passing so the husky younger man turned his head slowly and looked malevolently at Ben Moore. As the man's gun was flung away, striking the iron stove with a loud noise and skittering, Ben stepped directly behind the disarmed man.

The cook finally came to life. In a stentorian roar, he said, "Marshal, what in the hell do you think you're doing?"

Calahan approached the table, still aiming his six-gun, and asked where Jess Hearst was. The cook pulled up irately on his bench. "Over at the house. What'n hell would he be doing in here this time of night? You want him, go—"

Calahan was already speaking to the younger man. "What's your name? Where is your partner?"

The beefy man leaned back very slowly, freed his cup and studied Calahan. "Name's Art Fielder. My partner's over at the bunkhouse, as far as I know."

"What were you doing at the main house?"

"Talking' to the gent who hired us."

Ben Moore brushed the beefy man's neck with a cold gun barrel. "Empty your pockets."

Art Fielder leaned to arise, and Ben punched him with the barrel. "Sit. Just empty them."

Fielder began to methodically dump the contents of his pockets atop the table. The cook watched, looking increasingly indignant by the moment. When Fielder had finished, the other three men stared at some badly sweat-crumpled old folded greenbacks, some dully shining silver coins, and four gold coins of double-eagle denomination. The cook raised his eyes first, beginning to quizzically scowl at his coffee-drinking companion.

Ben stepped to one side to see the coins better. Marshal Calahan let his gun barrel droop slightly. "Where did you get the gold money?" he asked Fielder.

The cowboy answered shortly. "From Mister Hearst. Don't ask me why he pays in gold coins. Ask him."

Calahan considered the stranger. "Paid you for what? That's a lot of money."

Art Fielder looked at the pile in front of him and seemed disinclined to reply until the cook made an observation in a slighty suspicious tone of voice. "Jess don't pay in gold. His paw did, but Jess don't. I know, I been workin' here for seven years."

Fielder saw them studying him and shrugged. "All I know is that when he hired us on he said he'd pay for a couple months in advance and gave us some of them double eagles. Marshal, I don't ask a man where he got the money he pays me with."

Calahan agreed with that. "Most likely you don't. I'll ask you again: what did he pay you to do?"

Fielder went silent again and sat gazing at his personal things. Whatever other virtues the stranger had, being able to think fast in a sitting position was evidently not one of them. He had a characteristic of remaining silent at critical moments until someone jogged him.

Ben rapped him lightly on the shoulder. "What's your partner's name?"

"Joel Manning."

"You were in the saloon in town this morning, then you bought supplies at the general store."

Fielder sat looking at the tabletop.

"And you went south to an old ranch with a couple of other Hearst riders, and one of you shot a man named Morrison."

Fielder still sat like stone.

Calahan approached the ranger rider, put his gun barrel under the man's chin and forced his head up. When their eyes met, the marshal was quiet, but afterward, while increasing the gun pressure, he spoke harshly.

"Which one of you shot the man out yonder who was with us? You, your partner?"

Fielder had to tip his head farther back to avoid painful pressure. His bulging eyes met Calahan's cold, dark gaze. "It wasn't me."

Calahan stepped clear and holstered his Colt. He was still staring at the stranger when he addressed the cook. "Just stay in here, be quiet. Don't stick your nose where you hadn't ought to when we take this son of a bitch out of here. You understand me? Stay put, Jobey."

The cook's earlier furious indignation had become eroded by subsequent events. He had been jugged in Marshal Calahan's jailhouse a number of times for being drunk and disorderly on Saturday nights, so Jobey really had no particular feelings of fondness for the lawman. But he was stone-sober now, and whatever in the hell had caused this sudden appearance of the marshal and a companion armed for bear did not seen to be anything very minor. He growled as Ben Moore got the stranger to his feet. "Awright. It's none of my business, except somebody's goin' to pay to fix that back door."

The cook's last couple of words were completely lost in a violent burst of gunfire out in the yard somewhere. He was so startled he almost upset his chair.

Calahan grabbed his prisoner and gave him a violent shove toward the rear door. Ben hurried after them. He turned once to look back. The cook was pushing his suety weight between a huge old cast-iron cookstove and the protective log wall.

Calahan allowed Fielder no opportunity to make a rush for it in the darkness. He gripped him by the shoulder from in back and swung southward.

The gunfire ended as abruptly as it had started. After the last echo had gone there remained an acidy smell of burnt blackpowder in the still air.

Ben worried about Joe Benour. That had sounded as though at least three men had been simultaneously firing. Something had gone wrong.

The light at the main house went dark so rapidly it could only have done that if someone had rammed a bucket down over the lamp because oily wicks did not snuff out that fast. Ben leathered his gun, followed Marshal Calahan as far as the three-sided smithy, and when Calahan hurled his prisoner into the darkness there, Ben heard the man groan and curse as his shin struck an oaken anvil stand.

The smith was thick with layers of black forge soot. It had the typical smell of a blacksmithing works. What light was coming from above made absolutely no impression inside the old log shed.

Ben could make out Calahan and Fielder, but across the yard where all that gunfire had erupted, visibility was only marginally better.

The bunkhouse door was closed, he could make that out, and the place was no longer lighted. Now, in fact, there were no lights showing anywhere.

But what kept Ben motionless was the silence. There was not a sound of any kind, until Calahan snarled his prisoner to the ground and employed a length of light chain used as a kickstrap on recalcitrant horses being shod to secure Fielder to the massive old anvil atop its even larger round of cured oak wood.

Something vague, little more than an abrasive whisper, came across to the front of the shoeing shed from what Ben assumed was the direction of the barn. He swore aloud in spite of himself. Someone was making his way to the barn. There were three saddled horses tied out back. Even if whoever was making a desperate attempt to flee did not see those animals, there were other horses and more saddles over there.

Ben spat words over his shoulder as he started to move. "They're tryin' to get horses." He was already moving when Marshal Calahan squawked a curse and leapt over his bound prisoner to hurl himself at Moore.

They struck the ground together. Ben, expecting nothing like this, had half the breath knocked out of him. By the time he could suck in enough air to swear, someone with a Winchester peppered twice in the direction of the open front of the shoeing shed. Ben pressed flat to the ground, trying to locate orange muzzle blast. Calahan rolled away, pushing up his gun hand as he did so.

The Winchester did not fire a third time. Ben looked at the marshal. Whatever had occurred at the bunkhouse had evidently been beyond Joe Benour's ability to prevent Jess Hearst's riders from getting out of the building.

Moore heard Calahan huskily say, "lay a shot down through there when I run."

Ben cocked his gun, watched, and the moment Marshal Calahan came up off the ground in a dark blur Ben fired. He aimed high, and he fired more than once. He did not want to inadvertently hit a horse.

CHAPTER 21

A Long Night

CALAHAN made it. Moore's gunfire had driven the men in the barn to cover. As Ben saw the lawman disappear in darkness down the south side of the barn, someone inside used a Winchester to fire toward the front of the shoeing shed again.

This time Ben saw muzzle fire, aimed a little lower and fired twice, then had to roll a couple of yards and reload lying flat in the darkness.

The Winchester did not fire again. For as long as was required for Ben to shuck out empty casings and plug in fresh loads from his belt, there was not a sound. He rolled in the direction on the shoeing shed for cover, got to his feet over there and beat dirt and dust off with his hat, then peered inside and caught his breath for a long moment, walked toward the massive old anvil on its oak round and pushed Fielder with a boot toe. The man was dead. Ben had to kneel and look very closely in the darkness to find the hole in Fielder's head above the eyes and about midway between them. It was a small hole, the kind a Winchester .25–.35 made.

Someone whistled from behind the barn. The sound rose eerily then stopped. Moments later there was one solitary gunshot from a handgun. It sounded like a cannon, which made Ben suspect whoever had pulled the trigger had been inside the barn.

He edged up to the front of the shed, waited, and when someone over there whistled again, Ben made a crooked dash. He stopped against the barn's south wall, felt his heart hammering, faced westward and made out the corral with

162

the horses in it. They were having fits after that last, close gunshot, running, snorting, bumping one another. Ben began a slow stalk along the wall toward the rear of the barn. He did not see Calahan but he got abrupt evidence that he was back there when that man inside the barn fired again with his handgun, and this time there were two answering shots, so closely spaced they sounded almost like one continuous gun blast. Someone squawked in alarm inside the barn.

"Jesus! They got him!"

Ben stopped moving, decided Calahan did not need reinforcements and turned back toward the front of the barn. The men inside were concentrating on the rear. He sidled along the front wall to the upright balk on the south side, knelt to peer inside, and if two men hadn't been moving, their clothing lighter that the darkness, he would not have seen them. He fired four times as rapidly as he could cock the hammer and let it fall.

Somebody screamed.

Calahan opened up from out back, slanting shots because he dared not get around to fire straight up.

Ben had two slugs left. While he was trying to decide to fire them, a second Winchester opened up from the lower end of the yard. He did not see the first red flash but twisted in time to see the second one, take quick aim and fire back.

His gun was empty. He was sweating like a studhorse as he shucked out casings and groped for refills from his belt. If anyone had come out of the barn right then they could have cleaned his plow with a fence slat and he knew it. He prayed for Calahan to open up again. Instead the Winchester behind him at the main house stitched four bullets into the log wall. If that was Hearst, he was firing blind. None of his bullets came close. Ben was raising his handgun to fire back when Calahan's voice broke the deathly silence.

"Come out of there! Leave your weapons inside! One at a time with your hands on top of your heads! *Now!* Eight guns out here. You come out or we're goin' to drag you out by the heels. *Come out!*

Calahan sounded convincing, even when he lied about there being eight armed men with him.

Ben thought he glimpsed shadowy movement on the porch at the main house, so he held steady and fired three times, once ahead of the movement, once behind it, and once directly at it. He could not see through gunsmoke and darkness, but he heard a noise that sounded like a Winchester striking wood.

Inside the barn a man yelled at Calahan. "We're not goin' to do no such a damned thing. You're going to shoot us."

The marshal answered angrily. "No one is goin' to shoot you—unless you *don't* come out."

"Who'n hell are you?"

"Marshal Calahan from Wileyville."

Ben could hear the men at the lower end of the barn talking, but he could not make out what was being said. He faced forward again, leaned with his cocked handgun and called out, "You heard the marshal. We're goin' to ground-sluice if you don't walk out back."

Someone said, "All right. Marshal? You gave your word."

Calahan sounded disgusted when he replied. "No one is goin' to shoot you. Now come out there!"

Ben could barely distinguish them as they moved from different areas of the barn toward the rear opening. He ran back to the south wall and went down it fast, and when he reached the corner he stopped, trying to locate Marshal Calahan. He failed so he raised his handgun and leaned around until he could see the barn doorway. Three men emerged, hands on heads, looking left and right, moving warily.

Calahan allowed them to clear the barn by about fifty feet, then ordered them to lie facedown with their arms shoved out in front as far as they could reach.

Ben tried to find the marshal by his voice and failed again.

Calahan was in no hurry. He called to Moore. "Ben? You hear me?"

Moore answered shortly. "Yeah."

"Go back around front and down through. If they left one inside be damned careful."

Before Ben could turn, one of the men who'd gone on his knees before stretching out spoke to Calahan. "There are two dead men in there, that's all."

Calahan said, "Go look anyway, Ben," then he addressed the prone men in starlight. "What was all the shootin' about at the bunkhouse?"

The same gravelly voice replied. "Someone come up close, opened the damned door and commenced shooting. We didn't have no warning. He killed the range boss before a couple of us got set to fire back. Then he wasn't there. Ducked around to the side, I guess. . . . We came over here to get horses."

"One man scairt four of five of you?"

"Marshal, that wasn't just one man. He was as tall as the door, dressed all in black, an' when he opened up he bellowed like a bay steer. Then he was gone."

Calahan walked down from north of the barn. Ben had not expected him to be north of the rear barn opening. Calahan leaned over each prone man, then straightened up to reload his six gun.

Ben called quietly before moving into plain sight. Calahan glanced up, then finished reloading. When Ben halted beside the facedown men, Calahan said, "Who was that at the main house?"

Ben shrugged. "All I could make out was a shadow. Hearst, more'n likely."

"You get him?"

"I don't know. I think so."

"I'll truss these bastards. Go see if you got him. Be careful, there might still be one around here. The partner to the prisoner over in the shoeing shed."

Ben said, "He's dead. Shot through the head by a Winchester slug. . . . I'll be careful."

As Ben was turning to pass behind the outbuildings on his way toward the main house, Joe Benour stepped out in front of Moore and said, "I'll go with you."

Calahan called. "Hey . . . Joe?"

"Yeah."

"What happened? Where were you?"

"We'll talk about that in the morning, Marshal."

From the corner of his eye Ben studied the tall man in the Prince Albert coat. When they had to pause before crossing a moonlighted open place he said, "How many are left?"

Benour answered calmly. "Two dead in the barn, one dead in the bunkhouse, and maybe you hit someone over yonder. I'd guess them three in the dirt out back are all that's left. Still and all, you wait alongside the west wall of the house until I can skin down the rear and get on the east side of the porch. We can do a sight better comin' up onto anyone from both ends with them in the middle. And Mister Moore, don't talk. If you see him, shoot him."

After they reached the west side of the house Moore watched the tall saloonman depart with long strides. Benour had probably given him good advice. Of one thing Ben was certain: Benour shot first.

He did not disapprove of the idea except that shooting like that would eventually get someone killed who might not deserve it. Especially on a dark night. Ben hitched at his shellbelt, scanned as much of the front of the main house as he could make out below and behind the overhang, and thought there was a fair-sized lump east of the front door on the porch floor, but unless he could get closer he could not be sure what it was, even though he suspected it might have been the man who had dropped the Winchester.

He eased over to the north corner of the house, tried hard to make out what that lump was on the porch, palmed his six gun and was about to move when Benour's dry voice called softly from the opposite end of the porch. "There's someone lyin' up there. Keep your gun on him, I'm goin' up there."

Ben raised his Colt and waited. It was even harder to make Benour out, in his dark attire, than it was the lump. He moved around the side of the house, leaned down on the porch and waited.

Benour was moving, which made it easier for Ben to make him out. He knelt, remained that way for a moment, then spoke aloud in his natural tone of voice. "Ben, you got him. Come on up."

"Hearst?" Ben asked, while moving to climb onto the porch. Benour did not reply. He was rolling the man onto his back. When Ben arrived, the saloonman looked up. "Yeah, it's Hearst, and he's not dead. But I suspect he will be shortly if we don't get him down to town."

Ben sank to one knee. One of his slugs had hit Jess Hearst high in the body on the right side. There was blood everywhere. Benour shook his head. "I'll go tell Marshal Calahan. To save this son of a bitch we got to hitch up a wagon and start for town damned soon."

Ben pushed back his hat. Hearst seemed to be unconscious. One thing was clear even in the darkness: Hearst had lost a dangerous amount of blood.

Ben cut his shirt open, went inside the house hunting for clean rags and returned with a new white shirt that he cut into pieces to make a compress-bandage. He leaned back, wiping his hands waiting for the blood to show through. A little did, but evidently the compresses in front and behind were doing what they were supposed to do. Ben returned to the kitchen to rummage for whiskey. He found some brandy and took that back with him. Getting several swallows down Jess Hearst was difficult. Ben spilled more than he used but Hearst weakly swallowed.

Ben heard a commotion down at the barn and turned to look. Part of the noise was Benour and Calahan grunting as they pushed a light wagon toward the front tie rack in front of the barn. More noise was the result of one of them entering the horse corral for a couple of harness animals. The horses ran in panic.

"Moore . . ."

Ben swung around. Hearst was looking at him, breathing rhythmically but shallowly. He appeared to be marshaling his strength before speaking again.

Ben leaned to speak. "You're pretty well trussed up. Most of the bleeding's stopped."

"I should have had Fielder kill you," Hearst muttered.

Ben nodded. "Yeah, instead of Morrison. Why did you have him shot?'

"Morrison? Couldn't depend on him. If he got the arrowhead, he'd try to beat me to the cache."

"Well, Fielder's dead, so are your foreman and two other men. Calahan captured Manning and a couple more. By the way, the marshal already has two of your men in his cells; the ones who were hidin' in a ditch west of that abandoned old ranch. . . . Hearst—where is the arrowhead?"

The cowman had to turn his head to rid his mouth of blood. "Get me to Doc Pittinger," he muttered.

"They're rigging up a wagon. We'll be on our way directly. Where is the arrowhead?"

Hearst's eyes stared straight up at Ben Moore. They seemed dry. Ben got two more swallows of brandy down him. He weakly coughed but his eyes moved, then returned to Ben's face. "It won't do you no good."

"Why? Whoever puts the two together—"

"Still won't do you no good."

"Why won't it?"

"Because . . . my paw found that old cache years back. It had two boxes full of double eagles, part of some raid or other the Indians made. . . . My Paw brought back pieces every few months. After Paw died I tried to find it on my own."

"How did he find it without having both arrowheads?"

"He . . . had 'em. . . . That's how he found it. But he lost one. I figured you either found the arrowhead or you knew where the cache was—that's why you wanted the Oakley place."

"Hearst? Can you hear me?" Ben leaned down to test for breathing. It was there, but weak and fluttery. He put a hand on Jess Hearst's shoulder. "What made you think there was anything left? Maybe your paw got it all."

He had to lean to catch the reply. "Maybe . . . but I had to find out. The double eagles Paw left . . . were running out . . . gave some to Manning and Fielding . . . what's left . . . in money boxes at the house. . . . "

Hearst lost consciousness. Ben heard steel wagon tires grinding through dust. Joe Benour was driving. Marshal Calahan was standing in back, looking toward the house. At his feet in a thick bed of straw were three men with arms tied and three dead men rolled in blankets.

Ben arose. "Hang on," he told the wounded man. "We'll get you to town."

Ben went into the house for a blanket to use as a stretcher for Jess Hearst. Inside, he found Hearst's bullion box.

It was getting cold; evidently dawn was not far off. With a little luck they should arrive back in Wileyville shortly before sunrise.

CHAPTER 22

Wileyville by Dawn

DOCTOR Pittinger was making coffee in his kitchen while it was still dark out. His intention was to make breakfast later, after the Oakley boys awakened. He was an early riser and always had been. He had tried to break the habit without any success, so he had a couple of cups of java and awaited daylight.

It gave him an opportunity to consider events in a clear, calm frame of mind, so he did not really object very much that he'd been unable to break the early-rising habit.

He was at the table with his coffee, the kitchen was pleasantly warm from the cookstove, and because at this predawn time of day the world was usually still and quiet, he picked up the sound of a wagon while it was still above town. He listened, raised the cup and thought of freighters, who were also early risers.

The sound grew louder. Not just from the wagon but from chain tugs on the team horses. He took the cup with him, crossed through the dark parlor and stood at a window.

The sky was brightening over in the distant east to a pewter hue of dull color. The wagon halted out front. There were horses tied to the tailgate. One man was riding, two more were on the high seat. He watched one of them climb stiffly down and push through the little picket gate.

He stared from the mounted man in the Prince Albert coat to the wagon and the man still sitting on the high seat, then recognized the man coming toward his porch. Marshal Calahan!

Doc left his cup on a table, opened the door before Calahan rattled it with a gloved hand and stared. Calahan's clothes were disheveled, soiled, and badly wrinkled. Doc's gaze flicked back out to the wagon; he had a bad feeling in the pit of his stomach as Calahan stood on the porch.

"Jess Hearst's lost a lot of blood," Calahan said. "Maybe you can save him. There's three dead ones in the wagon and three for the jailhouse. We'll bring Jess in. The others we'll store in the jailhouse until you can get around to fixin' them for burial."

Doctor Pittinger glanced past Calahan again. There had obviously been one hell of a fight. He nodded at the Marshal. "All right. Bring him in. I'll light some lamps and leave the door open to the examination room. . . . Anyone from town get hurt?"

Calahan was turning away when he replied. "No."

Pittinger lighted lanterns and was waiting in the examination when they brought Hearst in. Doc took one long look at the cowman's face and made a little clucking sound as Calahan, Joe Benour, and Ben Moore placed the unconscious man on Doc's wooden table. He moved in beside the high wooden table, ignored the three men and felt for a pulse. There was one, but just barely. Doc went to work. Benour, Marshal Calahan, and Ben left; they drove down to the jailhouse, where Calahan locked up his prisoners and with help from his companions unloaded the bullion box and got the bodies of the dead men laid flat out in his storeroom. Ben and Benour took the rig down to the livery barn, where a wide-eyed hostler leaned over the side staring at the bloddy straw.

Out front, Benour pulled off his gloves, pocketed them, gazed up the road in the direction of his saloon and said, "I'm not goin' to get much sleep but I'm goin' to get some. See you later, Ben."

Ben did as he had done at the Hearst place, he watched as the tall man crossed the road heading for home, black coat swaying, tall figure resolute in its stride, and blew out a big breath as the livery barn hostler came up behind him with a question.

"What happened? I know them horses and that wagon. . . . There's a hell of a lot of sticky blood in the hay."

Ben lost Benour in the shadows and turned to face the hostler. "Goin' to be a nice day," he drawled and struck out for the rooming house at the north end of town. The hostler called after him. "Hey, mister—what about all them horses?"

Ben called back. "Given 'em plenty of feed, put 'em in a corral by themselves, make sure the trough's full. I'll be back later."

The hostler watched Ben continue northward, then went back down the runway to care for the animals.

Behind the steamy café window with its leaden glow of a lighted lamp, Elizabeth looked out. She knew her brother, Ben Moore, and Joe Benour were back in town because one of the toothless old gaffers who spent most of the day playing toothpick poker in a dingy corner of the saloon near the pot-bellied stove had told her. How he knew they had returned to town Elizabeth did not ask; she was too relieved to inquire.

As she prepared to open for breakfast, though, she occasionally watched across the road for signs of life at the jailhouse. There were none, the big padlock was still in place on the front door, and her brother had not arrived for breakfast. Those things heightened her interest but not her anxiety. If, as the old man had said, they had not returned to town until shortly before dawn, she was satisfied that they would be sleeping.

Job Upton from the stage company's corralyard accompanied by one of his yardmen, Slim Denham, arrived late for breakfast. Elizabeth would not have been interested in that fact if she had not heard a little of the conversation that passed between them. She did not hear much, just that Upton was annoyed over something he'd heard at the general store:

Jeff Hoffman, who had quit because he had said he did not like the hours, had gone to work for Jess Hearst.

Slim's comment about that was dry. "He's been complainin' ever since I've know him, so let him try cowpunching for a while, then he'll really have something to complain about."

"But he's no rangeman, Slim."

Slim chewed and swallowed before saying anything about that. "Jess Hearst must have thought so or else why would he hire the old fool?"

Upton changed the subject. "I went huntin' for Tom Calahan last evening to get some answers about what happened out at that old ranch. . . . Couldn't find him. Someone said him and two other fellers left town on horseback. Slim, I got a feelin' something is goin' on."

The yardman glanced up as Elizabeth loitered, smiled at her and responded dryly to his employer again. "Yeah. There's always somethin' going on."

Elizabeth returned to her cooking area, brushed hair back from her forehead and went to work dishing up several more plates of food. The next time she went down the counter to deliver platters of breakfast and glanced out the window, which was no longer steamed over, she saw her brother unlock the jailhouse and enter. She watched for several moments. From the north Ben Moore came strolling along. From the south Joe Benour crossed the roadway on a slanting angle in the direction of the jailhouse. Benour and Ben met in from of her brother's building, paused to say something to each other, then they too entered.

Elizabeth's worry atrophied but her curiosity deepened. Someone calling for a refill of his coffee cup distracted.

A little cold wind came from the northeast to stir dust in the roadway. It also somewhat mitigated the warmth that was just now beginning to make itself felt.

Elizabeth was taking empty plates back to her kitchen when a particularly lively gust of wind arrived, making her building creak and groan on its fir-log foundation. There were only three or four breakfast customers still at the counter. They ignored the gust of wind but Elizabeth raised her eyes to the roadway where tan dust was horse-high and swirling.

Through the obscured visibility she saw a horseman riding southward with wind at his back and dust nearly obscuring him. She stood rooted, empty plates in both hands. The rider turned his head once as he went past. He was wearing an old shapeless hat crushed down low to keep it from being carried away by wind. The collar of his blanket-coat was turned up. His horse was moving along tail-tucked and head down.

Her heart missed a beat. She had seen that old face many times but not for more than a year now. *Old Fred Oakley!*

She put the plates down, moved around the counter and went to the door. Rising wind created more dust, so much in fact that Elizabeth could see no farther than about a hundred feet southward.

There was no horseman. She braved the wind by opening the door to step out, raise a hand to protect her eyes from stinging dust and peer southward. There was no rider in the roadway, at least not as far south as the general store. Beyond that it was impossible to make anything out because of the dust. Even the buildings on the opposite side of the road were obscured.

She returned to the counter to complete cleaning up after the breakfast diners. It had been an illusion; whoever that horseman had been, it most certainly could not have been old Fred Oakley. She went to the kitchen, put aside the plates and leaned on the wooden sink. Why could it not have been the old man? He had turned his head just once, in the direction of her café. She had seen his face. The only thing missing had been that little pipe old Fred had rarely been without. But the face belonged to the old man, dust or no dust!

CHAPTER 23

A Windy Day

THERE was a big cloud of dust accompanied by a bitingly cold wind. At the jailhouse Tom Calahan closed and barred the alley door and rummaged for a handkerchief to wipe his watering eyes. He hated wind. A man could make a fire if it was cold. If it got too hot he could find a creek and soak in it, but what in the hell could a man do about wind?

Ben and Benour were already inside. They stood in silence gazing at the old-time bullion box at their feet. Ben made an observation that was probably totally alien to the thoughts of his friends. "It don't look like it was in the ground for all those years."

Benour sighed. "I've heard about those caches of buried treasure since I was a child. I heard about this one the first month I was in Wileyville. I didn't believe it then an' right now, lookin' at the box, I still got doubts. Tom, if this box's been buried maybe fifteen, twenty years, how's come it isn't rotten? Oak rots fast when it's buried."

Calahan had thought about a number of things on the ride back to town from the Hearst place, including the bullion box, so he said, "Joe, I'll bet money it wasn't in that hole the old man dug out. Look at it. . . . My guess is that old man Hearst used that box for his safe. However he brought the loot home, he didn't do it in that box. My guess is that he put it in there later."

Benour nodded. "You're maybe right. But one thing's sure: unless Jess makes it, we'll never know. . . . You got a crowbar?"

Calahan had one leaning against a wall among other tools. Without speaking he got it, shoved the tip through the padlock's loop and leaned. Nothing happened. Ben Moore moved over to grasp the bar and add his weight. The lock flew apart. Benour knelt, lifted the lid and remained silent and motionless as his companions came over to also look. The box was less than half full of gold double eagles. Benour said, "Maybe we should be surprised there's any left. Old Charley Hearst paid bills with those things since I been in the country." He picked up a handful of the coins and let them trickle back atop other coins in the box. "And Jess," he said. "He knew about the box. He'd been using the coins too." Benour leaned to begin counting. Ben and Calahan watched for a while. Calahan eventually went out front to his office to fire up the stove and put the coffee pot atop it. When he returned Benour had finished. He and Ben were quietly talking.

"This is a fortune," Ben said to Benour. "Most money I ever saw all in one stack in my life."

The saloonman made a thin smile. "Me too." He accepted the mug of hot coffee Calahan handed him. "Make a guess, Tom."

Calahan shook his head.

"Well," Joe Benour said, raising the cup. "Twenty-seven thousand dollars in gold eagles."

Calahan did not raise his cup, he stared at the money. He was shocked and showed it. "I wonder how much was buried to begin with?"

"If the box was full," opined the saloonman, holding the cup close to his mouth, "I'd say at least twice this much. Tom? The way I heard that story, Indians raiding down into Mexico buried their loot out yonder. Well, Mexicans wouldn't have that many U.S. double eagles, would they?"

"No, I wouldn't think so."

"Then them Indians didn't just raid into Mexico. Maybe they never raided down there. Maybe they raided up here. Is there anyone around who would know?"

Calahan wagged his head. "I doubt it." He sipped coffee.

"Must have happened over fifty years ago. What matters now is . . . what do we do with it?"

Ben Moore, who had only a few silver coins in his pockets—all the money he had in the world—made a suggestion. "You think we could ever find out where it came from—who it belonged to?" Neither of his companions thought that was likely. He drank half the coffee and put the cup aside. "Joe . . . ?"

Benour looked at him, then at Marshall Calahan. "This is just an idea," he said and hung fire before continuing. "That son of a bitch tried to shoot those little boys because he thought he could find the rest of the cache on their land. He would have stole their ranch too if Ben hadn't come along to put a kink in his tail. . . . Tom, half should go to them—put in the bank—an' us three divvy up what's left."

Marshal Calahan stood a moment looking at the box, then drained his cup and addressed Ben Moore. "Are you going to stay around?"

"Yes. I never figured not to. I own the Oakley place. For the first time in my life I own something more than a horse and a saddle."

"Are you going to keep the boys?"

"Yes. We already got a name for our partnership. The Arrowhead Cattle Company."

Calahan met Joe Benour's steady gaze. "All right. Half to the boys, with Ben here to be responsible for the money and the lads."

Benour made one of his rare, thin smiles. He nodded his head without saying a word until he had finished the coffee. "What'll we tell old nosy Custis at the bank?"

Calahan's dark eyes hardened. "We'll tell the pot-bellied old goat it belongs to the Oakley boys, and Ben as their guardian will have authority to use what they need to stock their ranch and put the place back into shape. An' if he gets nosy, I'll personally tell him that's all he's got to know, an' if he don't take the hint, I'll find a way to straighten him out."

Benour laughed. Ben was startled. He would have bet new money the saloonman did not know how to laugh. "You want me to go up there with you when we put the money in his bank? He don't care much for me, Tom. It's mutual."

Calahan's eyes twinkled. "All right. All three of us go up there. Now then, divide the money, put their share back in the box and . . ."

Someone opening the roadway door and slamming it after himself interrupted Calahan. He looked briefly startled, then turned on his heel, left the storeroom and closed the door.

From over near the front wall his sister said, "You didn't come over for breakfast, Tom."

Calahan stared at her, walked behind his table, motioned her to a chair as he sat down and said, "We run into some trouble out at the Hearst place."

She nodded. "I know that much. Jess Hearst is dead."

He looked steadily at her until she explained. "Doctor Pittinger was in this morning for breakfast. He was late. He said the reason for that was that he'd been doing everything he knew to do to keep Jess Hearst alive, but he died anyway."

Calahan's gaze drifted to the gun rack, hung there for a few moments, then went back to his sister's face. Calahan wanted a lot of answers. He had relied on the fact that Hearst might survive being shot to get them. Now, hell's bells, he would never get them.

"Tom?"

"Just thinking, Liz. You want to know what happened out there?"

"Are Ben and Mister Benour all right?"

He looked at his sister. "They're fine. Maybe like me a little sore, but fine."

She sighed. "What a relief. Now tell me what happened last night."

He started at the beginning and told her everything right up to the moment he, Ben, and Joe Benour had decided what to do with the cache of gold coins.

Her eyebrows went up. She looked in the direction of the storeroom door. "They are . . . in there?"

"Yep. You want to see the money? There are three dead men on the floor."

She shot up out of the chair. "No. Doc asked me to look in on the boys because he's got some embalming to do. I better get up there." She eyed the closed door again. "Mister Custis's eyes will pop out of his head, Tom."

The marshal was arising from behind his table when he said, "It's his darned long nose that bothers me, not his eyes. He's a real busybody. I guess that goes with being a banker."

"What will you tell him?"

Her brother smiled, said nothing as he came from behind his table and held the roadside door open for her. He still did not answer her question as she passed out of the office and he closed the door gently behind her.

When he returned to the storeroom Ben and Joe were waiting. They had put half the money back into the oak box, and what remained they had divided into three stacks. When Calahan walked in both Joe and Ben picked up a stack of coins and pocketed them. They made Ben's britches sag. He hitched at his belt but neither he nor the saloonman said a word. They waited for Marshal Calahan to go over and pick up the remaining stack of coins, then Benour said, "You ready to go up the back alley to the bank?"

Calahan was ready as soon as he pocketed his share of double eagles. The wind was still gusting as they started up the alley carrying the box between them, with Calahan walking in front. He fished for his handkerchief to mop his eyes again.

He was still doing this when they reached the barred alleyway door of the bank. He rapped with his knuckles. When that got no response he struck the door with his six-gun butt, hard. When the door opened, Bart Custis and his clerk with the green eyeshade and black sleeve-protectors were both holding shotguns. Calahan lowered his handker-

chief. "Put those damned things down," he growled and
shouldered past the clerk, who closed and barred the door
after everyone was inside.

Custis was a paunchy older man with very little hair, a
round, pale face, and small green eyes. He watched Moore
and Benour place the bullion box on a table. Then he
scowled at Marshal Calahan. "Most folks use the front door,
Marshal."

Calahan did not respond. He opened the box, waited until
the banker and his clerk recovered, then said, "For deposit,
Bart. Put three names on the account. Ben Moore, Jamie
Oakley, and Arthur Oakley."

Custis approached the box and blew out a long breath.
"Christ. That's gold money." He looked up. "Where did it
come from?" Then, before anyone told him, he straightened
back looking dumbfounded. "There really was a cache on
the Oakley place? Hell, I never believed that old story. And
those lads found it? I'll be damned."

Neither of the three younger men said a word, but as the
banker gestured for his clerk to take the box up front to be
counted, Ben and Joe Benour exchanged a solemn wink.
Marshal Calahan smiled at Bart Custis. "You know how
you're to set up the account?"

"You just told me, Marshal."

"Good. You take care of it. Ben'll be along later if there
are any papers to sign." Calahan jerked his head, led the way
out through a small wooden gate to the front of the bank
and did not stop until the three of them were out front in
the windy roadway. Calahan raised his handkerchief to his
eyes again as he said, "Joe, is your place open?"

Benour looked across the road and southward, fished a
large brass key from a trouser pocket and said, "It will be in
ten minutes. Come along." As he was unlocking the door he
also said, "Was that your sister come in the office, Tom?"

"Yeah."

"You told her everything?"

"Yep."

Benour shoved his spindle doors inward, leading the way to the bar. It was dingy inside the saloon. It was also redolent of stale tabacco smoke, horse sweat, human sweat, and spilt whiskey, but at least the wind could not come in. Benour went behind his bar, took an unopened bottle of pure mash whiskey from a shelf, opened it and set up three jolt glasses. "That damned banker made up his own story." They laughed as Joe filled the little glasses.

Calahan raised his glass. "To Jess Hearst. He's dead."

Ben and the saloonman were surprised by the news of Hearst's death. Ben, for one, had privately believed Hearst would not make it but he'd seen others pull through when they seemed to be goners. They drank to the departed cowman and Joe refilled the glasses. This time Ben let his glass sit there untouched. Benour noticed but said nothing as he leaned on the bar gazing at Marshal Calahan. "Remember that story I was goin' to tell you, Tom?"

"Yeah. I already heard it, Joe. . . . That's what happened at the bunkhouse last night, isn't it?"

Benour's gaze at the lawman was stone-steady when he answered. "Yep. Tom, you want to preach me a sermon about no-good sons of bitches deserving a chance?"

Calahan's black eyes shifted slightly so he could see the back-bar shelves of bottles. "No. When you walked away from us out back of the barn last night, I knew in my heart that's what was goin' to happen."

"And . . . ?"

Marshal Calahan lifted his jolt glass, emptied it and put it down. "I wish that damned wind would quit. Makes my eyes water every time. There aren't many things in this life I don't like but wind is one of them. . . . There are a couple more: biting dogs and kicking horses."

"You want a refill?"

"No thanks. Do we owe you or is this on the house?"

Benour was still leaning and looking steadily at Calahan. "On the house."

The lawman smiled. "I got to get someone to haul those dead men up to Pittinger's embalming shed. Ben, don't forget to go over to the bank."

Ben nodded. "I won't. I'll do it on my way up yonder to see the boys."

Calahan thought about that before speaking again. "You going to adopt them?"

"Your sister asked me the same thing. I don't see any need for it, Marshal. We're partners. That's what counts, not signing some damned piece of paper."

Calahan did a rare thing. He reached, slapped Ben Moore on the shoulder and turned to leave the saloon. After he was gone Benour straightened up off his bar and pointedly stared at Ben's untouched glass. "Mister Moore, that's pure malt liquor all the way from Missouri."

Ben eyed the little glass. "An' if I drink it, Mister Benour, I won't be able to find my rear end with both hands."

Benour refilled his own glass and hoisted it, then waited. Ben sighed, saluted Benour with his raised glass and downed its contents. Then he too left the saloon.

CHAPTER 24

Fixing to Start Over

BEN Moore was not a drinking man but he knew for a fact that about the time he reached Pittinger's little front gate that imported Missouri mash whiskey was going to take hold.

He was almost right—it hit him after he'd knocked on the door and about the time Elizabeth Calahan opened it. He smiled at her, squinted slightly for better focus, and as she moved aside for him to enter, he began having a detached feeling as though his feet and legs took him past the door and the handsome woman without his urging. While she closed the door and had to lean to secure the latch, he removed his hat, took down a big breath and as she turned he smiled at her—and could not think of a single thing to say.

She eyed him thoughtfully, did not return the smile and jerked her head. He followed her out to the kitchen where Jamie and Arthur were having supper with Doctor Pittinger. It was obvious from Elizabeth's place at the table that his arrival had interrupted her meal. He made an expansive gesture for her to sit down and finish. Doctor Pittinger was staring at him as the Oakley boys beamed and both spoke at the same time. The were not only glad to see him, they were excited about something else: Doctor Pittinger had told Arthur he could leave town and return to the ranch tomorrow, if he wanted to.

That is what they were both telling Ben at the same time. He laughed at them, and they laughed back. Doctor Pittinger's eyes had not left Ben's face. Until Elizabeth said the boys could be excused, Doctor Pittinger did not settle back in his chair. "Drunk," he said, as soon as the boys left the room. "Sit down. I'll get you some coffee."

Ben obeyed, dropped his hat on the floor and looked brightly at Elizabeth. "I'll come for them first thing in the morning. I been lookin' forward to this day as much as they have."

She let him finish, then spoke quietly while wearing a solemn expression. "I saw their grandfather."

Ben's bright look faded. He did not take his eyes off her as Doctor Pittinger placed a crockery mug of steaming black coffee in front of him, then went back to his own chair and sat down. "Where did you see him?"

"Right here in town, riding southward down Main Street at the height of the dust storm."

Before Ben could speak Pittinger said, "I told her in that kind of dust it could have been anyone. When a person can't see things clearly their mind plays tricks on them."

She ignored that remark and, without taking her eyes off Ben, repeated, "I saw him, Ben. I was looking out the café window when he came up even with the window and looked straight at me. . . . There was wind, yes, but very little dust. I know it was old Fred. Over the years I got to know him very well."

Pittinger cleared his throat, raised his cup and eyed Elizabeth skeptically over the rim of it.

Ben gazed at the tabletop. He was sober. His reason for not quite doubting her was because in the back of his mind he had often wondered if the old man might not return. Intuition—a lingering hunch—inclined him to believe he had returned and Elizabeth had seen him.

He reached for the coffee cup. "Riding south, you said?"

"Yes."

The coffee was hot so he put the cup down. The ranch was west, not south. He changed the subject. "Is Arthur strong enough, Doctor?"

Pittinger seemed relieved that the conversation had taken

a different turn. "I think so. Once we got decent food into him, along with warmth and the rest, he came along better than I expected. Just don't let him overdo it. Make certain he's kept warm and dry. Don't let him get too tired. Feed him all he'll eat. . . . I'll drive out in a few days."

Ben told Doctor Pittinger what he had told Elizabeth, that he would be after the boys in the morning, right after breakfast, then he stood up holding his hat, thanked his host for the coffee and said, "Figure out what your bill is an' I'll pay it before we leave town."

Doctor Pittinger became resigned. "One of these days, Ben. One of those times when I drive out."

Ben dropped a golden double eagle atop the table, smiled and left before Pittinger recovered from the shock and asked questions.

Elizabeth remained behind to explain. Doctor Pittinger examined the coin closely before pocketing it and saying what other people had said, "You mean there really was a cache out there?"

As Elizabeth arose from the table she buttoned her coat against the wind, smiled, patted Doctor Pittinger's hand and left the house, bracing for the wind, which was no longer blowing.

Her brother came to the café when he saw her unlocking the roadway door. She pointed toward the kindling box. Marshal Calahan dutifully fired up the little iron wood stove while his sister draped her coat from buck antlers in the kitchen and fired up the cookstove. When she returned to the counter, the café was warming up and her brother was patiently waiting for coffee, which she got him and waited until he had tasted it before speaking.

"Ben and the boys are returning to the Oakley place in the morning."

Calahan raised dark eyes. "The littlest one is well enough?"

"Yes."

Her brother sat relaxed with the cup between both hands,

looking thoughtful. "I talked to the prisoners one at a time. That feller called Manning knew quite a bit. It seems Jess didn't send Fielder to the old Brittany ranch to shoot Ben. He was to shoot Morrison because Jess figured Morrison was going to be troublesome, which most likely was the truth. But Jess did send the other pair to shoot Ben. According to Manning, Jess had to get rid of Ben to get at the Oakley boys so he could claim the Oakley place. They were to shoot him and get the arrowhead."

Elizabeth did not seem surprised at any of this. She crossed both arms and gazed out the roadside window. Marshal Calahan watched for a while, then said, "Did Ben give you an arrowhead?"

"Yes."

"Well, there's supposed to be another one somewhere around. Maybe out at the Hearst main house somewhere. But I don't know that this is important now because a person can dig to China out yonder in that thicket and never find anything old Charley Hearst hadn't already dug up. . . . Elizabeth?"

She was motionless, arms crossed, gazing over her brother's head out the window. She slowly met Tom's gaze. "Yes?"

"You're not interested in what happened, are you?"

"Yes, I'm interested, but I'm more concerned about Jamie and Arthur. They have a lot of money now. They and Ben will build up their Arrowhead Cattle Company. Your prisoners at the jailhouse will stand trial when the circuit-riding judge arrives, and Jess is dead along with some other unsavory individuals."

Calahan continued to look up at her. "All right. You've got it pretty well worked out the way it's goin' to be. . . . What else is on your mind?"

"Jamie and Arthur."

"You just said they got plenty of money and a partner to build up the ranch with them. What more do they need?"

Her gaze drifted back to the window. "The old man, Tom.

Old Fred. I don't know whether they need him or not, but I do know he is here. I saw him in the roadway." Her gaze went to his face. "Why did he come back after abandoning them? What does he want?"

Marshal Calahan looked into his empty cup for a moment, then arose from the counter as he said, "It'll be up to him, Liz—if you really saw him."

Her dark eyes flashed but she retained control. "I saw him, Tom. I know I saw him."

Calahan smiled at her. "All right. Well, I got some papers to write over at the jailhouse. The circuit rider will want them completed when he gets here." As he was leaving, he turned back at the door still smiling. "Maybe next week we can hire a rig from Henry an' drive out to the Oakley place."

She watched him cross the road, then went to her cooking area to be ready when the next drove of hungry men arrived. Because there was no front-wall window in the kitchen she did not see Ben Moore walking past in the direction of the general store.

He had been down to see about buying a light wagon from Bullerman, who had several rigs for sale or trade. What Ben ended up with was a light team of driving horses as well as their harness and the wagon. His intention was to purchase enought provisions at the general store so that he would not be required to return to Wileyville for a long time.

He spent a lot of time and money, selecting and buying supplies. He went up to the harness works, bought two saddles with thirteen-inch seats, bridles and blankets to go with them, and just before leaving to get the wagon and drive it up for the supplies, he also bought two new hemp thirty-foot catch-ropes. Jamie and Arthur had a lot to learn. He grinned to himself about this, then went after the rig.

While he was out front loading supplies with the help of a clerk from the general store, Alfred Pittinger happened along. He leaned over the side to examine what was being loaded, and when Ben came out with a carton of tinned stewed tomatoes Pittinger said, "What's the shotgun for?"

Ben got the tomatoes settled before replying. "Sage hens, rabbits, maybe quail and the like. Anything is better'n a busted slingshot, and the boys like to hunt."

Pittinger continued to lean. "I got a hunch it's going to be a long time before all the details of this mess are cleared up."

Ben nodded. "Yeah. My feeling is that a lot of it never will be cleared up. Not with Jess and his paw dead. That arrowhead Arthur found beside that sunken place where Charley Hearst dug up the cache—why was it there? My guess is that the old man either dropped it or tossed it away after he found the cache. He sure didn't need it anymore."

Pittinger looked thoughtful. "Sounds reasonable," he said. "Wasn't there supposed to be another one?"

"Yes. Maybe the old man already had it. Otherwise how would he know where to dig for the cache? But that's one of those things we're goin' to our graves wondering about."

Pittinger straightened up off the wagon side. "Not me. I liked Charley Hearst but the rest of it—how he knew where the cache was, when he dug it up, and how that arrowhead happened to be there for the lad to find—Ben, long ago I learned not to worry over things I'd never find answers to. Just you remember what I told you: keep the lad warm, don't let him get overtired . . . and where did you get that double eagle you paid me with?"

"Didn't Liz tell you? Maybe I'd ought to let you wonder. Naw—we found a bullion box hidden in the house. It had quite a few of those coins still in it. I'd bet my life that's the money from that cache old Charley found over on the Oakley place."

Pittinger smiled. "See you in the morning. I'll have the boys bundled up."

Ben moved aside so the store clerk could ease a crate of tinned provisions from his bony shoulder to the wagon's tailgate.

Later, Ben drove up to the harness works, loaded the youth-sized saddles, the lariats and other articles, then turned back down in the direction of the livery barn, where he intended to leave the rig until morning.

After his conversation with Doctor Pittinger he had speculated about whether Jess had known his father had found the cache before the old man had died. If he hadn't, then it was reasonable to assume that Charley Hearst did not trust his son, and that seemed likely if what what Jamie and several other people had told him about the relationship between father and son. But again, he would never know. He spat over the side, made a wide yaw to enter the livery barn runway with clearance on both sides and smiled to himself. Doctor Pittinger had hit the nail plumb on the head. There was no point in speculating about things a man would never know the answer to.

None of that was really important anyway. What *was* important was what he did with the rest of his life, beginning tomorrow.

Henry Bullerman came out of his little office as Ben hauled back to a halt and slackened the lines before going down the near side of the loaded wagon. Henry said, "Well, didn't no wheels fall off, did they, an' them horses didn't bolt with you, did they?"

Ben shook his head. "Nope. But if any of that'd happened, I'd have less cause to worry than you would have."

Henry made an uncertain smile, leaned to look in at the load and wagged his head. "You're fixin' to set up in business for a long while I'd say."

Ben handed the lines to the liveryman. "For life, Mister Bullerman."

"Henry. Remember when we first met I told you my name was just plain Henry?"

Ben remembered. "Yeah. Henry. Tell me something, Henry: Tomorrow when we pull out I'll tie my horse and the gray mare to the tailgate. What we're goin' to need, though, is maybe three or four more good using stock horses."

Bullerman's face brightened. He rubbed both hands together. "Ben, this here is your lucky day. A short while back I traded for six head of genuine using stock horses. Not too old neither. In their prime, as they say. Sound too. Come out back an' I'll show them to you."

Ben did not move. "Can't right now, Henry. But if you still got em in about a week from not I'll sure be interested."

Bullerman's brightness faded. "A week? Ben, I trade an' sell horses. I don't keep no horse a week if I can peddle him." Henry thought a moment, then said, "But I'll tell you what I'll do. You come look at 'em. Try 'em out if you like, an' if you buy 'em I'll put 'em over across the alley in my holding corral an' feed 'em for a week for you—free."

Ben turned toward the back of the runway. "Let's go see them."

That was how Moore acquired the additional using horses he and his partners would need, but as he was counting out payment he told Bullerman he'd need for him to feed them for maybe *two* weeks because Ben wasn't sure he'd have time to come to Wileyville for them in less than that length of time.

Henry was holding half the cash in his hand as he listened. Ben went on counting out the full amount, then stopped counting and looked up.

Henry smiled. "Two weeks it is. You made a good stroke of business, Ben. I know for a damned fact them is as good a set of cow horses as I've ever had in my corrals."

Ben smiled, reset his hat and walked up the back alley instead of returning to the front roadway. He didn't stop until he was at the Pittinger place. Doc opened the back door for him. Arthur and Jamie were at the kitchen table eating bread and milk, except that it looked to Ben as though Arthur's bowl had cream in it instead of milk.

He declined the medical practitioner's offer of food, told the boys what he had bought from Bullerman and what he had bought at the harness works, then winked at Doc Pittinger at their speechlessness.

CHAPTER 25

Settling In

THEY left Wileyville with dawn chill in the air and arrived at the ranch with late autumn heat somewhat mitigated by a high, hazy overcast.

This first day back, they spent the day until supper time dunging out. There wasn't much left of the wood rat's abandoned nest but they burned the remains.

They stowed their grub in kitchen cupboards, made that bedroom with the old bedstead in it suitable for Jamie and Arthur, and with sunset fading went down to the barn to park the rig and look in on their four horses. The animals were hungry. Ben led his horse out to be hobbled and turned loose, then did the same with the gray mare. She knew about hobbles, so he brought out their harness animals next. They too understood what hobbles were and went hopping after the other two horses out where the grass was strong.

The boys lingered longest at the saddle pole in the barn, touching the two new saddles, inhaling the good scent of leather, and when Ben said they'd have to try out those rigs tomorrow, adjust stirrup leathers and all, Jamie and Arthur beamed.

The boys bedded down after supper. When Ben finished in the kitchen and tiptoed in to look at them, they were sleeping like logs.

He went out front for a smoke. It had been an eventful day and he was tired, but it was a good kind of tiredness. He ambled out to look at the horses. Bullerman had not said whether either of the light-harness animals was a combination horse. Most horses their size were. In the morning he'd have to saddle them up one at a time and find out because

192

he had two partners, they had two riding outfits and only one saddle horse, the gray mare.

He smoked, listened to the night, and gazed northward in the direction of the Hearst place. He had in mind going up there shortly to find rebranded Oakley critters and bringing them back with him. About the Oakley horses he was not at all hopeful.

He speculated briefly about the person who would take over the Hearst place, finished the smoke and went inside to bed down. The house smelled of cooking and wood smoke, things it probably had not smelled of in over a year.

In the morning the boys were anxious to go down to the barn so they ate fast. When they finished Ben pointed to the big dishpan with hot water in it. Now would be as good a time as any for them to learn that partners shared.

By the time they reached the barn that hazy overcast he had noticed yesterday was gone. In its place was a flawless azure sky and a climbing, warm sun.

He brought the horses in, rigged out one of the harness animals, led it out into the yard, cheeked it and swung. The horse rolled its eyes, humped up a little and waited. Ben squeezed it with his knees and reined left. The horse moved out in that direction. It reined fairly well, and while it did not act as though it was accustomed to the saddle it certainly had been broken to ride. He took it back, tied it out front, rigged out his horse and the gray mare with the new outfits, boosted Arthur atop the mare, helped Jamie mount his horse, spent fifteen minutes lacing stirrup leathers to the right length for both boys, then grinned up at them. "Walk. Just walk. Stay beside me, one of you on each side."

That was how they left the yard. It was also how they returned almost four hours later. Ben was satisfied that both boys had done their share of horsebacking when they came down to the front of the barn and dismounted. He left them to care for their animals but watched. Arthur's short legs created difficulties but each time he looked at his brother or

Ben as though for help, Ben said, "You're on your own, partner."

That evening he steered them into helping with supper and afterward in cleaning up the kitchen. It had been an easy, pleasant day. None of the things he had hoped would not happen had happened. "Tomorrow," he told them, "we're goin' cattle hunting."

It required three days, not one, to locate rebranded Oakley critters and drift them back where they belonged. They had thirty-five head, which was, according to Jamie, fifteen head less than there should have been. Ben jutted his jaw in the direction of some obviously calvy cows. "They'll make up for it come spring."

Arthur said, "Are we goin' to rebrand 'em right?"

Ben watched the animals plodding ahead. "Maybe next spring, Art. We got 'em back. I don't think anyone's goin' to claim them, and we got other things we got to do before full winter arrives."

Jamie looked around. "Like what?"

Ben was entering the yard when he replied. "Cut firewood. Winter's not far off. In fact it should be along any day now. We need lots of firewood to see us through."

They used the wagon, "made wood" in the foothills and camped for three days until the wagon was loaded with split and quartered rounds, then they went down-country toward home. Ben seemed never to be in a hurry. He watched Arthur closely and set his pace and the times of rest to the youngest boy's stamina. Otherwise they could have returned much earlier with a loaded wagon.

They had the wagon tailgate a couple of feet inside the woodshed and were unloading and stacking firewood when Arthur raised up from pushing out wood, stared westerly, then said, "Hey. Somebody's coming."

It was Elizabeth riding alone and without haste. She had plenty of time to see what the partners were doing before she reached the yard, halted over at the barn, tied up, then walked up to the woodshed. Arthur leaned over the sideboard glowing with pleasure. She stood on tiptoe and kissed his cheek. Jamie smiled, kept a small distance between them and shoved out his hand. He did not want to be kissed. At fourteen-approaching-fifteen something like that was not just embarrassing, it was demeaning.

Elizabeth was wearing a split-hide doeskin riding skirt and a light tan blouse. Ben Moore wiped off sweat and gazed at her. It hadn't been much more than a week but she looked more handsome than he remembered.

She smiled back. "You haven't wasted any time, have you?" she said.

"Can't," piped up Arthur. "We got to lay by five or six cords to get us through the winter."

She turned slowly toward the younger boy, who was standing in the wagon bed. "I rode out because of you, Arthur." She brought forth that oversized old arrowhead from a pocket and held it up for him to take. "I didn't want you to be without your lucky piece."

Arthur thanked her and examined his talisman briefly before pocketing it. When she turned back Ben had not taken his eyes off her. He said, "Fellers, how about heading for the kitchen and makin' up a pot of coffee?"

Jamie helped his brother down and shortened his pace to that of his little brother as they walked away. Elizabeth and Ben watched them go. Elizabeth looked up at him. "Jamie is so protective."

Ben nodded. "Yeah. I expect it's pretty much always been like that between them." He met her gaze. "That was decent of you to remember his arrowhead and bring it out."

Her gaze faltered, then she said, "Henry Bullerman is wondering when you're coming for those horses you bought from him."

"I told him two weeks."

"Ben, it's been almost two weeks."

He smiled. "Time sure flies, don't it?"

"Yes. In fact it's been twelve days since you left town." The moment she said this she turned slightly and reddened, something he did not notice, then she said, "Tom and I could bring the horses out if you're pressed for time."

He took her by the hand and led her into fragrant woodshed shade. "We couldn't ask you to do that, Liz. You got the café to run and—"

"I have an offer to sell it."

He stared. "Sell the café? What would you do?"

She lifted a piece of wood from the tailgate and pitched it toward the back of the shed as she answered. "There are other things. Cook for some cow outfit, for one. Or maybe leave the country, find something else to do."

He reached with a gloved hand to sweep dust and splinters off the tailgate, then hitched around to sit on it. He patted the rough old wood. She sat up there beside him. Her view was limited to the stacked wood along the back wall but she studied it as though stacked firewood was something she enjoyed looking at.

He considered her profile in long silence, then said, "Liz . . . ?"

She did not stop gazing at the stacked wood. "Yes, Ben?"

"Well . . . I can't cook worth a darn. I never could. I got a hunch Jamie and Art aren't goin' to grow up being any better at it."

She continued to sit there looking toward the back wall of the shed. "Sound's like you want to hire a cook, Ben."

"I wasn't thinkin' about a cook, Liz."

She met his gaze calmly. "Oh?"

He fidgeted on the tailgate and reddened. He was sweating. He had heard about her disillusionment with men. He also remembered how head-on hostile her first glance at him had been. If those things were not inhibiting enough, he was also aware that the unsettling thoughts he'd had about her lately were things he lacked experience in expressing.

She interrupted his uncomfortable silence by saying, "Ben?

Has it occurred to you that the boys, especially Arthur, will need more than saddle horses and cattle as they grow up?"

He gripped the edge of the tailgate as he nodded his head. "Yes'm. Schooling and knowing other kids and—"

"And mothering."

He let go a rattling breath. An' mothering . . . Liz?"

Her dark eyes softened with a touch of ironic humor. This time the man was neither glib nor confident, he was awkward and clumsy. "You could find a wife," she said.

He peered at the scuffed toes of his boots below the tailgate. He was really sweating now. "I expect so. . . . I haven't met many women since I came down here."

She made a soundless sigh. "You only have to meet one, Ben."

He fished for his blue bandana, lifted his hat and mopped off sweat, then he took the bull by the horns. "I only know one I'd want to think about like that." He stuffed the bandana in a pocket and reset the hat, then faced her. "You."

She returned his gaze without a waver. She had been thinking that this would be hard work, but she had not expected it to be *this* hard. She smiled. "I love this place. I used to ride out and Marybeth would go with me. We'd ride for miles. Sometimes we'd take the boys with us." She paused and brought her eyes back to his face. "Are you sure you'd want me out here?"

He looked at her round-eyed. "More than anyone in the world. I got to tell you something, Liz. I've been head over heels in love with you since that first day I saw you, and you glared at me."

She offered her hand. He took it and tightly held it. "You didn't show it, Ben."

"Scairt to."

She squeezed his fingers and softly laughed. "I need to know something. Are you asking me a question, Ben?"

He thought about that. "Yes'm. I'm askin' you to marry me."

She leaned until her head was on his shoulder. "All right. That' will make four partners in the Arrowhead Cattle Company, won't it?"

He was turning toward her when Jamie called from the house. "We got dinner ready. If you don't hurry up it'll get cold."

Elizabeth slid off the tailgate, eyes twinkling. "You said they don't know how to cook."

"They don't. This is goin' to be something."

She tugged him along. "Act like it's the best meal you ever ate." He winked and grinned as they crossed the yard. He squeezed her hand, and she squeezed back.

CHAPTER 26

A Gray Horse in Shadows

HE and the boys brought the new saddle stock back from Wileyville. They had to go back to the foothills for another load of wood but first he wanted to try out the new animals, so he rode them out, worked them on the rein and brought them back. He could not fault the first two. Jamie and Arthur were vigorously cleaning their new saddles, which did not need cleaning, as he rigged out the third horse, led it forth and climbed aboard.

He walked the horse for a mile, then boosted it over into a lope. It was an easy-riding animal, did not shy when a rabbit broke cover almost beneath it, and as he turned off north-westerly in the direction of some low hills, the horse went willingly, interested in new country.

They veered behind the nearest low hill and rode up a long, wide slot behind the hills. Ben liked this horse and talked to it as he did his own horse. The animal flipped his ears back, then forward. He also raised his head. He had detected a scent. Ben tipped down his hat for eye shelter and studied the countryside. There was a stand of spindly jack-pines atop the low hill dead ahead. From up there it would be possible to see a long way southward, easterly and west-ward.

There was a horse tied to a low pine limb up there. Ben might have missed locating it if it had been almost any color but gray.

His first thought was that it might be a Hearst rider, although that was very unlikely. The ones Calahan did not have in his jailhouse were dead. Unless there was one who had eluded detection.

Ben reined closer to the hill, rode in shade for a half mile, then hobbled the horse and started climbing. It took time; he went from one stand of underbrush to another. By the time he was near enough to the topout for a good look at the gray horse he also saw an upended saddle in the short grass and what seemed to be a meager camp.

He freed the thong that held his six-gun in its holster, worked his way through a flourishing stand of brush and raised up very slowly until he had a clear view of those jackpines and the flat ground around them.

The gray horse either detected movement or picked up manscent because it came out of its doze, raised its head with little ears pointing in Ben's direction and stood perfectly still.

He finally saw the man on his knees rolling some blankets. For five minutes Ben remained completely still. When the man had finished with his blanket roll and had tied it, he arose.

Elizabeth had been right!

Ben shoved out of the thicket, the man heard him doing this and took several steps forward until he could see out where there was no tree shade.

Ben walked ahead. They stared at one another until there was no more than about twenty-five feet separating them, then the old man slumped and started to turn away.

Ben stopped him. "Hold it."

The old man stopped and turned. Ben was in shade when he said, "It *was* you. Elizabeth Calahan swore she saw you riding past during a windstorm a couple of weeks back."

The old man said, "I'm leaving. I'll be rigged out to ride in a little while. . . . Well, what do you think of the ranch you won in that poker game up north?"

Ben went to a tree and leaned. "Why did you do it?"

"Do what? Put the deed in the poker pot?"

"Abandon the little boys."

Old Fred Oakley looked at the ground. "My son died. He

was all I had in the world. He'd been my whole life since he was little an' his maw died. . . . He upped and died."

"And his wife."

Old Fred nodded sluggishly. "Yes, an' her too. . . . I couldn't stay. I couldn't stand lookin' at things him an' me built and worried over. It was all I could think about. Getting plumb away. Far away. I just had to go so I saddled up in the night and rode north. Always north."

Old Fred stopped explaining and raised his eyes. "It took a long time, mister. It'll be with me as long as I live. But last month I got to thinking about the lads. So I struck out from up north. . . . The wind was blowing something fierce when I reached Wileyville. I rode down through and headed for an arroyo I knew about and camped down there until the wind let up. Then I rode five miles out an' around so's I wouldn't have to see them buildings my boy and me built. And camped different places.

"I saw you and the boys. I been watchin' for a couple of weeks. More, I guess. You three would ride out. I seen the good-lookin' woman that has the café in town ridin' with you a time or two.

"The boys had new saddles. They was proud as peacocks. I even heard 'em laughin' a time or two. The oldest one looks just like my son, his paw. Mister, it was like twistin' a knife in my belly to see him an' hear him.

"Well, I seen all I had to see. Today I was goin' to head southwest, maybe go down through Arizona, maybe all the way out to California. I heard they got gold out there waitin' to be dug up."

Fred Oakley ran work-scarred bent fingers through his coarse, gray thatch and gazed at Ben. "I'm glad you came down here, mister. I'm glad you won the ranch. . . . Now then, I got to finish strikin' camp."

Ben watched the old man shuffle back where his rolled blankets were lying. He said, "Fred, listen to me. Come down there with me. The boys wonder about their grandpaw."

"No. Someday you can tell 'em, I guess." Fred turned. "I got to tell you, mister, I just couldn't stand it. Maybe especially in the evenings when my boy and I'd set on the porch and talk about what we'd done, and what we still had to do. . . . I couldn't look at that porch, at the house or the barn. . . . I'm sorry. Truly I am, but I just couldn't do it."

Ben watched the older man filling saddlebags and readying his gray horse to be rigged out and burdened. He rolled and lighted a smoke. "The boys will always wonder," he told the old man. "They'll worry."

"Naw, they're happy. I could see that a mile off. They're happier'n I could make them. Mister, I can't smile any more. I just plain flat-out don't have a thing to offer them. You do have.

"Maybe they'll never understand. Maybe they will. Mister, do them a favor, don't tell them we met out here until they're full grown. Maybe then they'll understand. They sure as hell wouldn't before that."

Ben ground the smoke out underfoot and walked over to help the old man raise his heavy saddle to the gray's back. They looked steadily at one another across the saddle seat. "You put a burden on me, Fred."

"I know, and I'm sorry about that. But if you'd just rode on past, it wouldn't have happened." The old man shoved his work-swollen hand across the saddle seat. Ben gripped it, with neither of them speaking, and when the old man got astride and reined westerly along the topout and turned once to wave, Ben waved back—with a lump in his throat the size of a rock.

He lay awake many nights afterward remembering everything the old man had said, and was never able to decide whether the old man had been justified in what he had done or not.

He did not tell Elizabeth about that meeting until they had been married six years, and it was another ten years after that before he told Jamie and Arthur.